PRIVATE
Practice

a **PRIVATE PLEASURES** novel

PRIVATE *Practice*

a **PRIVATE PLEASURES** novel

SAMANTHE BECK

Entangled Publishing, LLC
10940 S Parker Rd
Suite 327
Parker, CO 80134
rights@entangledpublishing.com

Brazen is an imprint of Entangled Publishing, LLC.

Edited by Heather Howland and Sue Winegardner
Cover design by LJ Anderson/Mayhem Cover Creations
Cover photography by deagreez1/Deposit Photos

Manufactured in the United States of America

First Edition February 2013

ENTANGLED
BRAZEN

To Charles.

Chapter One

"To be honest, I'm relieved Roger and I called off our engagement."

The snippet of conversation from the booth behind her pulled Dr. Ellie Swann's nose out of her medical journal. She blinked and stared at the large window beside her. Its reflection offered a view of the bustling interior of DeShay's Diner, including the booth where Melody Merritt and Ginny Boca huddled over pie and coffee.

Ellie forced her attention back to her journal and held her breath, waiting for the conversation to resume. No, Melody's broken engagement was none of her business, and yes, eavesdropping was wrong, wrong, wrong. But she couldn't resist listening in, because the discussion involved Roger Reynolds, the object of her longstanding and completely secret adoration.

"Roger and I weren't well suited. I know we looked like the perfect couple—high school sweethearts and all—but between college in Manhattan, and then law school and the clerkship in DC, he changed. He picked up big-city tastes in some, ahem, intimate areas."

Goodness. Ellie used her napkin to blot the sweat from her upper lip. *Like what?*

"What do you mean?" Ginny asked, her voice pregnant with curiosity.

Ellie flipped the page in her journal and feigned deep interest in an article about a recent drug trial for a female libido enhancer, of all things.

"He wanted me to—" Melody paused. Ellie peeked in the window and watched the blonde's reflection glance around the diner, scanning the area for prying eyes and ears. Wise move. Sleepy little Bluelick, Kentucky, might be a mere speck on the map, but it boasted a grapevine of staggering efficiency.

Ellie shamefully included herself in the prying eyes and ears category, but the real irony was Melody's choice of confidant. If the local gossips elected a president, Ginny would win by a landslide.

Apparently satisfied she had no unwanted listeners, Melody leaned toward Ginny and whispered. Ginny's mouth dropped open. Ellie strained to hear, but it was no use.

The statuesque blonde leaned back in her chair and shuddered delicately. "I am *not* that kind of girl. I just won't do those things. I mean, I like sex as much as the next woman, but Roger's looking for a nymphomaniac. His ideal woman has a whole lot of experience and very few boundaries." She sighed and shook her head. "I'll always love him, as a friend, but really, it's for the best."

• • •

Hours later Ellie stared at the moonlight slanting through the window of her cozy bedroom and reviewed the conversation she'd overheard at the diner. Her conscience cringed at the rudeness of eavesdropping, not to mention coveting another woman's freshly cast-off fiancé. Either transgression might explain why she was still tossing and turning at one thirty in the morning.

Let it go for the night, she told herself, but her stubborn mind refused to obey. Shadows played across the ceiling while she obsessed over how to turn her most cherished secret wish into reality. She'd had the dream, in one form or another, for as long as she could remember: Roger fell in love with her. They married, moved to one of the stately old houses overlooking the river, and lived happily ever after, preferably with a passel of blue-eyed, honey-haired mini-Rogers. Roger III first—they'd call him Trey—and then Michael, or Elizabeth, if they had a girl...

The low rumble of a motorcycle tore through the quiet of the warm June night, distracting her from her family planning. Abruptly, the noise ceased and silence reigned again, everywhere except between her ears.

Melody had headed the cheer squad in high school. She was beautiful, limber, and full of...pep. If Melody couldn't satisfy Roger in the sack, what chance did academic-minded, unathletic, and comparatively inexperienced Ellie Swann stand?

So close, and yet so far. On one hand, their paths seemed perfectly aligned. She'd recently moved back to Bluelick to open her general practice and keep tabs on her father, who was facing, or more accurately ignoring, a type 2 diabetes diagnosis—not that he seemed particularly thrilled with her weekly check-ins. Roger had returned home to join his family's law firm. They were both single young professionals looking for love. On the other hand, unless she transformed into a sexually adventurous woman, fast, he'd never give her a second glance.

Thankfully she wasn't still "Sparky" Swann, the sad little

dork she'd been in high school. Back then the most curvaceous thing about her had been the thick round glasses she'd worn to correct nearsightedness. The intervening years had brought the final flourishes of puberty, LASIK surgery, and a much-needed fashion intervention by her college roommates. Nobody mistook her for a Victoria's Secret model, but at least she didn't still look like a refugee from science camp.

What did Roger look like now? Letting her heavy eyelids drift closed, she conjured up his golden perfection in her mind's eye. She could picture him clear as day, seated in pew four at Bluelick Baptist with the rest of the Reynolds clan, all tall and square-jawed in his Sunday best. Would his eyes retain their stunning sky-blue clarity? Would he still have his star quarterback's body and thick, gilt-blond waves? It didn't matter. She adored Roger for more than his pretty container. Everything about him appealed to her, from his large, loving family to his sense of tradition and duty, confirmed by his decision to follow in the footsteps of his father and grandfather, joining them in their law practice.

In the seamless way of dreams, Roger turned to her and smiled his heart-stopping, almost blindingly white smile. The congregation launched into a booming rendition of "Rise Up, O Men of God." He winked and leaned in close. *Can I share a secret with you, Sparky? I'm—*

Something crashed, and a low, distinctly un-Roger-like voice muttered, "God*dam*mit!"

She bolted upright in bed, heart pounding. Her eyes automatically sought the red glow of her bedside clock: 1:47 a.m. Had her subconscious sound editor missed a cue, or had a real-life noise jarred her out of what had been shaping up to be a very interesting dream? Holding her breath, she listened intently, and then nearly screamed when another crash sounded from her front porch. Another muffled curse followed.

Her feet hit the floor. Her hand swept across the surface
of the bedside table, searching for her phone. The slow, steady
crunch of gravel betrayed someone's progress around her cute
and, gulp, *isolated* cottage. When the footfalls stopped, her
racing heart pole-vaulted into her throat. Someone lurked
outside her bedroom window.

Your open bedroom window, her mind screamed. What
had she been thinking, going to sleep without locking the
window? Now nothing but a flimsy screen and a wispy white
curtain separated her from some crazed rapist-murderer.
Unless this guy had the body mass of a mosquito, she was
screwed.

She snatched up her phone and ordered herself to calm
down. Bluelick wasn't exactly a hotbed for cold-blooded
violence. Everybody knew everybody and a good percentage
of them were related. If she braved a look outside, she'd
probably find some kid pulling a dare, more scared than she
was.

A deep, almost lazy "Hey, Doc?" broke into her weak
attempt at self-soothing.

The voice didn't sound like a kid, or the least bit scared.
Her fingers fumbled over the phone, tripping up the simple
9-1-1. If he wanted to come in, he'd be through the window and
choking the life out of her in less than a minute. Emergency
responders would reach her in time to draw a chalk outline
around her cold, dead body.

"I've got a gun!" she croaked, trying for Dirty Harry, but
sounding more like Kermit the Frog.

"Well, that's fine, Doc," the oddly familiar voice drawled.
"But you don't need it. I've already been shot."

Shot? Holy smokes, was he serious? She flicked on her
bedside lamp, but before she could formulate a response, he
went on. "C'mon Sparky, open up. I heard you moved back
home to hang out your shingle. Congratulations, you've got

your first patient."

That he'd called her "Sparky" didn't mean much. The entire town knew her by that godforsaken nickname, but her fear ebbed, because an unmistakable stitch of pain threaded her mystery visitor's voice.

She crept to the window. "Who *are* you?"

"Tyler Longfoot. Remember me?"

What woman could forget Tyler Longfoot? Four years older than her, a whole lot wilder, and monumentally cooler, Bluelick's very own badass rebel had always radiated dangerous charm. A vision of him floated through her mind: the devil's mane of thick, black hair; flashing green eyes filled with careless challenge; sensual lips cocked with wicked intent.

Pushing the curtain aside, she stared out. Sure enough, he stood there, a tall, rangy figure illuminated by the meager light from her bedside lamp. He wore his hair shorter now, but still a little untamed. It fell like a raven's wing over his forehead. Otherwise, ten years hadn't changed him much— or dimmed his bad-boy appeal.

"What the hell are you doing, slinking around my house at two in the morning?"

"Bleeding to death," he said, not bothering to keep his voice down. Why would he? He'd already woken up the only other person around. "I'm not kidding, Doc. I need your help." He leaned forward until the light fanned across his face, revealing pain-filled eyes.

"Why didn't you ring the bell like a normal person?"

"Because after setting off every damn booby trap on your minefield of a front porch, I figured I had about fifteen seconds to get 'round here and let you know who it was before you called the cops or put another bullet in me."

Her fingers automatically tensed on her phone. Okay, maybe his strategy wasn't completely incomprehensible.

Letting her gaze drift down, she tried to spot evidence of an injury. "You're walking and talking pretty well for a man who's supposedly been shot."

"It's a flesh wound, but it hurts like a mother—"

"All right. Go around. I'll meet you at the front door." He nodded and turned to go back the way he'd come. She grabbed her robe, shrugged it over her white nightie, and went to meet him. Along the way, her mind took an unscheduled trip back to sixth grade.

Even at twelve, she'd recognized that Tyler Longfoot oozed sex—hot, no-holds-barred sex—although at the time she wouldn't have used those words. She'd gotten an eyeful of Tyler kissing Melody's older sister, Melinda, behind the bleachers during a Bluelick Buffalos home game and had thought he looked like one of the rogues gracing the covers of the paperback novels for sale at Dalton's Drugs. He'd certainly seemed to kiss like one. He'd bracketed Melinda's slim waist with a lean, muscular arm, holding her close while the power of the kiss actually bent her backward. Ellie had felt light-headed and tingly just watching.

From the time she'd been old enough to daydream about happily ever after, she'd cast Roger in the role of Prince Charming, but seeing Tyler kiss had made her wonder what happened once the enchanted couple rode off into the sunset.

She flicked the porch light on and looked down. The garbage bags she'd placed by the front door in preparation to haul them to the end of the driveway tomorrow morning— well, later today—were toppled and the contents scattered. Into the mess stepped a pair of scuffed black work boots. They jutted from the fraying hems of well-worn jeans. Her eyes traveled up long, muscular legs, absently noticing worn-to-white stress points at the knees, along the creases near the front pockets...the fly. A picture of eager female fingers tugging those buttons invaded her mind.

Shoving the unhelpful image away, she continued her inspection. A white T-shirt stretched across the hard expanse of his chest and hinted at chiseled abs. A smear of something that looked suspiciously like pink lipstick decorated the collar, and some lighter imprints shimmered on the bronze skin of his neck.

When she reached his striking green eyes, she found them staring back at her, filled with equal parts pain and amusement. "Where's your gun, Sparky?"

"I go by Dr. Swann nowadays."

"Where's your gun, Doc?" A grin teased his lips.

She brought her hand from her robe pocket and stuck it out at him, index finger extended from her fist, thumb cocked. "Bang."

He staggered back playfully and then winced for real. "You got me."

"Where?" She still saw no trace of an injury.

By way of answer, he strode past her into the hallway. She turned to follow and immediately spotted the dark stain spreading over his hip pocket.

It wasn't a ton of blood, but enough to bring a twinge of apprehension. "Tyler…"

He stopped halfway down the hall. "Where do you want me?"

"In my office downtown."

"Funny, Spark—Doc."

She caught up to him and put a hand on his arm. His muscle bunched beneath her fingers. "I'm not joking. Better yet, how about the ER in Lexington?"

"No, no. Let's keep this between you and me. We go running into town, someone's going to see us. At the ER, they'll file a report of the shooting with the authorities."

She removed her hand and stepped around so she faced him. "That's going to happen anyway. I'm required to report any gunshot injuries to local law enforcement. If I don't, I put my license in jeopardy."

Without warning, he swayed and slumped against the wall. She grabbed him around the waist.

"Tyler! Tyler, do not pass out. You hold on to me, okay?" His arm around her shoulders felt reassuringly strong, and thankfully, his legs seemed able to support his weight. "Let's go to my kitchen, so I can take a look and see exactly what we're dealing with. Then I can decide where best to treat you."

She doubted he was lucid enough to follow her suggestion, so he took her by surprise when he guided them down the hall to the kitchen and hit the lights.

Her eyes took a minute to adjust to the sudden brightness. Once they did, she focused on her patient. His color was just fine and his pupils fully responsive. "Funny, I don't remember seeing you at the housewarming party."

A smile tugged at one corner of his mouth. "I built this house. I know the layout well enough."

"Oh." That rang a bell. Maybe her father or, more likely, one of the handful of former classmates she'd run into had mentioned something about Tyler starting a construction company several years back.

He stood in the middle of her tidy kitchen, looking incongruous and extremely masculine next to her lemon-yellow curtains and matching dish towels. Heavens, he was... something. The mature, logical voice in her head momentarily regressed to high school and squealed, *Oh. My. God. Hell-raising, cherry-popping Tyler Longfoot is standing in your kitchen, about to drop his pants.* Then she remembered why. Shaking off the disturbing mental lapse, she inched toward the door. "Let me get some supplies. I'll be right back."

Get a grip, Ellie. He's the one who should be feeling light-headed, not you. She hurried to the hall closet to retrieve her medical bag.

Slightly winded, she skidded into the kitchen and saw him standing with his jeans undone and hanging low on his hips, hands propped on her solid, butcher-block table.

"This work for you, Doc?"

Depending on the caliber of the bullet and where, exactly, he'd been hit, she could have a comparatively easy extract-and-stitch job, or something requiring sedation, an MRI, and a couple hours of intricate surgery. Better to keep him upright and theoretically mobile until she determined the severity of his injury.

"Yes, that's good," she replied in her best calm doctor voice. After scrubbing her hands in her deep farmhouse sink, she took a pair of rubber gloves from her bag.

She snapped them on, moved a chair into position behind him with her foot, and sat. Then she dug around in her bag and placed supplies on the table. When she had everything organized, she said, "Okay, I'm going to lower your jeans and shorts as gently as I can, but you might feel some tugging if any fabric adhered to the wound."

"Well, Doc, I'm behind on my laundry, so it's just jeans tonight. Hopefully that simplifies things." He twisted to look at her as he spoke, causing the jeans to sink lower. A heartbeat later she heard his quick intake of air as she pulled one side down to give her better access to the wound.

"Sorry. This could be painful. We should probably stop right here, slap a pressure compress on and call an ambulance."

"I'm fine, Ellie," he insisted through a clenched jaw. "Just do what you gotta do."

"Okaaay. Face front and be still." He turned around, and she concentrated on the matter at hand. Within a moment, she'd carefully probed the thin, fairly shallow line of the wound and located the...bullet? Pellet? She was no munitions expert. It was a small metal projectile, embedded about a quarter-inch deep in the spectacularly carved indentation of his buttock, between the gluteus medius and the gluteus minimus. But when she gently separated the margins of the wound for a better look, her patient sucked in a harsh breath.

"Son of a— Are you amputating half my ass back there?"

"Not yet. Don't distract me."

"Take your time." His clenched jaw didn't quite muffle the sarcasm.

She loaded a syringe with local anesthetic. "Can you count to three for me?"

"Sure. One, two—"

Ellie jammed the needle in and depressed the plunger.

Tyler swayed like a palm tree in a high wind. "Jesus *effing* Christ! What happened to three?"

Ellie pulled the needle out and placed it on the table. While waiting for the anesthesia to take effect, she explained, "Three is where you tense up and a little shot ends up feeling like a knuckleball hitting your muscle at ninety miles per hour."

"Oh, well, thank you very much. That felt like eighty-five miles per hour, tops."

"You're welcome." Using gauze, she dabbed blood away from the injury. "Let's give it a minute to work, and then I'll remove the bullet and you'll be as good as new in no time."

A skeptical grunt served as his reply.

She selected a long, slender pair of tweezers from the table and lightly touched the wound. No reaction from the patient. "Want to tell me how this happened?"

"Would you believe, self-inflicted?"

She laughed. "Not a chance. Nor will I believe your dog, cat, bird, or iguana accidently discharged your gun. Nor, at this hour, will I believe it was a hunting accident."

"Worth a try."

"Try the truth," she recommended, enjoying a moment of triumph as she snagged the small metal round between the tweezers and extracted it. She flushed the wound and pressed more gauze to the site.

He sighed. "I was down at Rawley's Pub, having a drink and, um, let's say *chatting* with Lou Ann Doubletree."

Lou Ann had been a year ahead of Ellie in school, but she remembered the tall, sandy-haired blonde well enough. The older girl boasted two particularly unforgettable features. "Lou Ann Double D?"

"For a girl who's not fond of her own nickname, you're awful quick to toss out someone else's."

"She *liked* hers. She was proud of the body parts inspiring it."

"They are inspirational, you gotta admit."

"So I'm told," she said, doing a mental eye roll. What was it with men and mammary glands? She tied off the thread on a surgical needle and prepared to start stitching. "So, you were at Rawley's, chatting with Lou Ann, and…"

"She's on-again-off-again with Junior Tillman. Remember him?"

The name sounded familiar. Her memory called up a wide, burly guy with a booming voice and a proclivity for smashing empty beer cans on his forehead whenever the Buffalos scored a touchdown. She completed the first stitch. "Beefy guy. Your year. Had a voice like a bullhorn?"

"That's him. Anyway, according to Lou Ann, they're currently off, but Junior showed up tonight with his drink most definitely on, and a slightly different recollection of where they'd left things."

"So he *shot* you? I can't believe you haven't already called the cops." Despite her agitation, she added another small, tidy stitch to the meticulous line. It would be a travesty to scar such perfection.

"No need to get all worked up. He went after me with the coon chaser he keeps in the gun rack of his pickup. He wasn't aiming to kill me, just stake his claim."

"Stake his... Oh my God, you're all hopeless." She tied off the final suture, cut the thread, and tossed the scissors on the table.

"Not my way of thinking, Doc. I'm just trying to explain what was going through Junior's half-rocked mind. He's going to feel real bad about this once he sleeps off the booze."

"He can sleep it off in a cell," she said firmly.

Tyler made a negative sound. "Junior's a damn good builder, plus he's got a four-year-old boy with a baby mama over in Ashland. If he's in jail, it's going to be real tough for him to make child-support payments. Then the kid suffers for Junior's bourbon-fueled bad judgment."

"He *shot* you. I'm obligated to notify the authorities. It's nonnegotiable." Considering the matter settled, she affixed a bandage over the stitches. "You're done."

He craned his neck to look at his bandaged cheek, then hauled up his jeans and turned around. Those hypnotic green eyes captured hers. His lips curved up in a slow, simmering smile. "Everything's negotiable."

Melody's words from the diner floated through Ellie's mind. *Roger's ideal woman has a whole lot of experience and very few boundaries.*

Practicing medicine wasn't a gig for the easily shocked, so she didn't see boundaries as an issue. But experience? That was another matter. Maybe the answer stood before her, in the form of a walking, talking wealth of sexual know-how? Medically speaking, he also qualified as a walking, talking female libido enhancer.

"C'mon Doc, what would I have to do to persuade you to keep this between us?"

Chapter Two

Tyler listened to the silence while his question hung in the air between them. Ellie stared for a moment and then gave him such a measuring look he actually felt heat crawl up his neck. What the hell was going through her mind?

"Since you were, shall we say, *chatting up* Lou Ann this evening, I take it you're currently unattached?"

Lou Ann had done all the chatting, in truth. He'd been looking for a polite way to shut her down even before her lips started blazing a trail along his throat, because Junior was one of his best friends and, contrary to what everyone seemed to think, he didn't make a habit of hitting on his best friend's girl. He crossed his arms over his chest and started to rest his hip against the table before remembering that probably wasn't a good idea. "Yeah, Doc. I'm still waiting for that special someone to come along."

"But you like to stay busy while you wait."

Her words held no hint of judgment. Rather, his own recent but steadily growing dissatisfaction with his revolving door of a love life caused the comment to stick in his craw. Or maybe taking a bullet in the ass for being stupid or just plain bored enough to hang around when Lou Ann had flirted served as a wake-up call. Either way, seemed like time to make a change.

"Some might say," he answered, eyeing her. This was an odd conversation to be having with anyone, let alone Sparky Swann. What in the hell did his relationship status have to do with convincing her not to report Junior to the authorities?

The belt of her short, pink robe claimed her full attention. "You're very experienced in a particular area where I'd like to increase my...um...competency."

She glanced at him, absently worrying her lower lip between her teeth. The gesture caused an uncomfortable tightening in his groin. "You want to learn how to build a house?"

"I'm talking about sex," she said, setting her lip free, so now it was just her deep, brown gaze grabbing him by the balls. "You've been honing your talents since you were a teenager. If the gossip can be believed, you enjoy a sex life most guys only dream about."

"Hey, now, you can't believe everything you hear." But a highly ambitious part of him begged to disagree. It begged him to part her slippery pink robe and show her things *she'd* only dreamed about.

This is Sparky Swann, he reminded himself, a bookish, awkward little girl, 'cept she didn't appear to be any of those things anymore.

"I only have to believe a quarter of it. Tyler..." She trailed off and dragged a hand through her long, dark hair, unconsciously telegraphing nerves. "Promise to teach me how to be a wild woman in bed and I'll leave it to some other concerned citizen to report Junior to the cops."

Maybe he'd been shot in the head tonight too, because something was definitely wrong with his hearing. "Sorry, what did you say?"

Her chin came up. "You heard me. I want hands-on, real-life instruction."

"Okay, let's back up a minute. Mind if I ask why you think you need to be 'wilder' between the sheets?"

Those bourbon-and-Coke eyes skidded away from his again.

"I'd rather not say."

"Of course not." Sighing, he stared at the toes of his boots and tried to get his head around her proposal. "Let me sum this up, just to be sure I understand. You agree not to notify the sheriff if I promise to be your sex tutor?" He glanced up at her.

When she nodded, he laughed. "That's pretty damn straightforward, Doc. Certainly strips all the silly games and romance out of the mix."

"Oh, come on. How is my proposal any different from you and Lou Ann hooking up at Rawley's on a random Friday night? You want it, she wants it, and off you go. You both know darn well the evening doesn't end with a bended-knee proposal. It's about enjoying the physical experience and then moving on. I'm suggesting the same thing, except without the drinks, small talk, or the risk of getting your ass shot off, and…"

Her words faded and her captain-of-the-debate-team expression shifted to a look he couldn't readily identify, but nonetheless made him feel like a jerk.

"And I'm no Lou Ann Doubletree," she observed quietly, wrapping her robe tighter and securing the tie at her waist. "How stupid of me. Look, if you don't think you can muster it up, forget I said anything."

Ah hell. "I never said I couldn't muster it up. Trust me. That's not the problem."

"Then what is?"

"Maybe I feel like a child molester, mustering it up for little Ellie Swann."

"I'm twenty-eight years old, hardly a child."

She had a point. The crazy cap of frizzy ringlets she'd never quite tamed as a kid had turned into a tumble of smooth, ebony waves. Pert features and dimpled cheeks had matured and refined, so the grown-up version delivered a one-two punch of sweet and sexy. Back in the day, she'd worn glasses so thick she could see into next week, but now, only big, brown Bambi eyes blinked up at him. And that mouth. Even bare, it looked soft and ripe and kissable.

"No argument there, Doc."

"Then what's the problem? I don't buy the ethical dilemma. If you can bang Double D for the fun of it, you can bang me."

"Let's get one thing straight. I've had sex with women, I've seduced women, and on rare occasions, I've even made love to women, but I have never, ever *banged* a woman." Still, terminology aside, he couldn't debate her conclusion. If she'd shown up at Rawley's tonight, a beautiful stranger, he'd have been first in line to offer her a drink, some small talk, and anything else she wanted.

Unfortunately, she wasn't some beautiful stranger. She was Ellie. He'd always harbored a soft spot for her. They'd both been raised by tough, remote fathers carved from the same cold, hard stone. And while as far as he knew, Frank Swann had never resorted to the beatings Big Joe Longfoot had loved to dole out for any actual or perceived transgressions, the man hadn't exactly showered his only child with praise and encouragement.

Taking in her big eyes, soft, sleep-tousled hair, and extremely kissable mouth, he realized he now had a hard spot for her as well.

The soft spot was easier to accept.

"Fine," she muttered. "Semantics aside, do we have a deal or not?"

Christ, how did he get himself into these situations? Pressing his thumb to the growing ache between his eyes, he begged, "Give me a minute to think. How many, uh, *tutorials* are we talking about?"

She pondered the question for a moment and he could almost hear the gears in her head turning as she calculated. "Ten?"

His dick shot up and shouted *Sold!*, but his sense of self-preservation kicked in with a lowball counter. "Two."

"Eight," she retorted, and he secretly appreciated her unoffended gamesmanship.

"Four."

"Five. That's my final offer. Anything less and I don't get enough education to make it worth risking disciplinary action from the state licensing board."

"Okay, done."

She smiled, and the dimples he remembered from years ago winked in her cheeks. When she stuck out her hand to shake on it, he fought a powerful urge to pull her close and kiss one of the adorable little dents. He'd never tutored anyone before, but this would be easy. Take her out a few times, give them both some thrills.

"Great." She reached into her black bag, grabbed a handful of something he feared might be condoms, and tucked them in the pocket of her robe. "Let's get started—"

His laugh cut her off. "No offense, Doc, but I doubt I can muster it up tonight. Half my ass is numb."

She pressed those full lips of hers into what she probably considered a stern line. He wondered how she'd react if she knew it had his dick springing to attention and proving him a liar.

"None taken," she said, and marched toward the door. "I

was going to say, let's get started once your stitches are out."

"Ah." The teacher's aide in his pants settled down. He followed her into the hall. "Sounds like a plan. How long before…?"

She reached into her pocket and handed him a packet of gauze and a couple of large bandages. "Change the dressing daily. Make an appointment with my office for Thursday and we'll see how the wound has healed." She halted at the front door. "If everything looks good, we can figure out a timeline and pin down the curriculum."

He nearly fumbled the supplies as he tucked them into the front pocket of his jeans. *The curriculum?* Leave it to overachieving Ellie to treat something as instinctive and elemental as sex like an academic pursuit. Though he couldn't explain precisely why, the notion of a specific lesson plan excited and terrified him at the same time.

"Let's not overcomplicate things. I'm comfortable winging it in this area."

She scrunched her brow in another expression he found an inexplicable turn-on and then shook her head. "*I'm* not. I don't want to waste one of my sessions covering something I already know. My goal is to expand my knowledge."

He fought an urge to wipe his sweaty palms on his jeans. "What, exactly, do you have in mind?"

"To be honest, I'm not sure yet. I need to do some research."

"You go ahead and *research* to your heart's content, Doc, but I reserve the right to veto anything on your so-called curriculum."

That stalled her. "Why?"

He stepped out onto her porch and turned to her. "'Cause I'm the expert." True, and yet the fact suddenly struck him as a little pathetic. She'd taken less than half an hour to decide the main thing he had to offer dangled between his legs. He had a sneaking suspicion most of the women in town would agree. Admittedly, he hadn't worked hard to cultivate a different impression, but he *was* good for more than tangling sheets. One way or another, he was going to prove it to her, if only for pride's sake.

Maybe it *was* pride, or contrariness, or maybe it had more to do with the sight of her standing in the doorway, looking at him dubiously and nibbling her lower lip, but he leaned in until he was close enough to see the subtle variations of color in her fascinating brown irises. "What do you say we start with a basic aptitude test?"

"A test?"

Her quick inhale reached his ears just before he brought his mouth down on hers. He'd meant to surprise her and perhaps throw her a little off-balance, but the surprise was all on him. The second he tasted those soft, velvety lips, all thoughts about proving anything except how fast he could get them out of their clothes, into bed, and rocking each other's worlds ran right out of his head. Along with any shred of caution and a good portion of his blood.

Her thoughts apparently raced down the same path, because she surged up on her tiptoes, clamped a hand around his neck, and returned the kiss with all kinds of innate talent. His mind went as numb as his butt. Before he knew what he was doing, he had his hand fisted in the slippery fabric at the back of her robe, holding her close while his tongue took a long, slow slide over hers.

An appreciative sound vibrated deep in her throat and she pressed even closer. The unguarded little noise penetrated the haze of need he'd sunk into the minute their lips had touched. He drew back, sucking in air like a drowning man, and waited for the world to tip back onto its axis. What the *fuck* was he doing? Getting shot and then propositioned had clearly screwed his equilibrium. There was no other explanation.

Her eyes blinked open and focused on him. In them he read all kinds of shock and awe, which would have been satisfying but for the disturbing fact that they mirrored everything currently going on inside him. He bit back a groan as he watched her tongue make a quick sweep over her lips, now wet from their kiss.

A tardy sense of self-preservation kicked in. He let go of her and stepped back, absurdly grateful his legs cooperated. When she wobbled and grabbed the doorframe for support, he felt some of the satisfaction that had previously eluded him.

"Congratulations, Sparky."

She shook her head as if to clear it. "For what?"

He couldn't have held back his smile if his life depended on it. She looked so discombobulated.

"You passed with flying colors. 'Night." He held on to the smile until she shut the door, and then all hell broke loose between his ears.

Cleaning up the mess he'd made of her front porch didn't bring him any closer to figuring out what had just happened. He'd kissed women. Plenty of women. Maybe more than his fair share of women, and enjoyed every single lip-lock. Some stood out, some faded into a background of pleasantly lustful encounters. None came anywhere close to that kiss with Ellie. It felt like hurtling into a new adventure and coming home at the same time.

The realization troubled him. He used his long strides to put some distance between himself and the biggest shock of his life since taking a bullet in the ass. He was supposed to be the one who knew what he was doing. But as soon as she'd parted her lips and applied herself, he'd realized this straight-A student was about to set the curve yet again. Hell, she'd set it, skewed it and then blown the damn thing away.

He carefully straddled his bike, more than a little grateful for the local anesthesia, and kick-started the engine. Fine. They'd struck a deal and he'd hold up his end, but before they dove into her so-called lessons, he'd take a few precautions. First, make sure the good doctor understood the real-life implications of what she thought she wanted. All the research and planning in the world didn't mean that when the moment of truth arrived, she wouldn't have second thoughts—especially if he planted one or two of them himself. If she did, well, he'd graciously let her out of the bargain.

Second, he'd find out why she'd hatched this crazy proposal in the first place. He had an uncomfortable suspicion that his eager student intended to use what she learned to blow the pants off someone else.

• • •

Ellie rattled off her request for a skinny mocha to the fuchsia-haired cashier at Jiffy Java. Normally, the word "decaf" would have preceded her order, but after her early-morning caller, she needed a jolt of caffeine. Her patient schedule was mercifully blank because her official opening wasn't until Monday, but she planned to spend her entire Saturday setting up three exam rooms' worth of supplies and organizing her office. These activities required some uninterrupted time... and energy.

She tried and failed to stifle a huge yawn as she moved to the pickup counter to wait for her order.

"Sparky, you haven't been back long enough to be bored to death already," a teasing voice intoned.

Turning, she came face to face with... "Roger! Oh my God, it's so nice to see you." *Nice* to see him? Could she be any lamer? She smoothed the hem of her slim black T-shirt and wished she'd paired it with something more eye-catching than cropped khaki cargos and black canvas ballet flats, because he looked wonderful. A pristine white polo shirt and tennis shorts set off his sun-streaked hair and tanned skin. Could any man be more perfect? And yet, even as she formed the thought, a picture of Tyler sprang into her mind—tall, dark, and distractingly handsome. She shoved his uninvited image out of her head.

"Good to see you too, Ellie." Roger's warm greeting and the quick brush of his lips against her cheek sent her heart fluttering. "Or should I say, Dr. Swann? I heard you were back."

Dazzled by his smile and the mesmerizing sparkle in his heavenly blue eyes, she managed a breathless, "News travels fast."

"'Round these parts, it doesn't have far to travel." With a shake of his head, he added, "I can't believe it's really you." He stepped back and took stock. "Sometime during the last ten years you got all grown up. You look good, Ellie. Really good. How are you?"

A blush heated her face, all the way to the roots of her hair. Thankfully, the barista placed her mocha on the counter just then, giving her an excuse to turn away for a moment. "I'm great." *Giddy, nervous, nearly incoherent with excitement.* "And you?"

"I'm doing well"—his smile faltered—"or, maybe I should say working my way in that direction. I don't know if you heard about Melody and me?"

"I heard you called off your engagement," she said, giving his forearm a comforting pat. No way would she admit to overhearing *why*. "I'm very sorry."

He offered her a pained look. "News travels fast, huh?"

She inclined her head and gave his earlier response back to him. "'Round these parts, it doesn't have far to go. But I have to admit the news came as a shock. I always assumed you two would go the distance."

He sighed. "She's a great girl, and she'll always be my best friend, but our relationship just didn't work out. I— It's completely my fault."

Sympathy swelled her heart. Melody might have been putting on a brave face for Ginny, but she hadn't sounded nearly this broken up about the end of the engagement yesterday afternoon in DeShay's. Frankly, she'd come across as completely at peace with the decision, whereas he seemed racked with guilt.

"If you need a good listener or a shoulder to cry on, I'm available." *I'm available?* Shoot, did she sound too forward? All she'd meant was—

"Thanks, Sparky. That's really sweet." His eyes shifted to someone behind her. He straightened and smiled. "Hey. How's it going?"

This time when she turned, she came face-to-face with her 2:00 a.m. caller.

His mouth tipped up at one corner in a slow, ridiculously sexy grin. "She doesn't like to be called Sparky anymore— prefers Ellie or Dr. Swann."

"Whoops. Sorry, Ellie. I hope I didn't offend you. It's just"—he shrugged—"you've been Sparky for as long as I can remember. Since the Knights of Columbus Annual Fourth of July Festival back in…gosh, how long ago was it?"

She prepared to brush the question away, but Tyler spoke up. "Twenty-two years. You were six, right Doc?"

Shock that he remembered the details of the incident nearly overshadowed her annoyance. Why in God's name did he have to have such perfect recollection of something she'd prefer to leave long forgotten? "Right. Six. Hardly a fair age to be saddled with a lifelong nickname."

"Well, you did burn down the bandstand," Roger pointed out with an apologetic smile.

"Blame Budweiser and Earl Rawley, who should have used better judgment, considering the man owns a pub. What kind of maniac hands a six-year-old a sparkler and then lights it? Small wonder I freaked out. Thank God nobody was hurt."

"I wouldn't say 'nobody,'" Roger objected. "I think your dad blew a vessel. I'd never seen anyone so mad before."

Yeah, he'd been angry. What Roger probably didn't appreciate, being only six at the time and from a family where no one ever raised their voice in anger, was that *she'd* been as much the target of her father's temper as Earl. Her little accident had forced him to actually deal with his daughter instead of pretending she didn't exist. A quick glance assured her Tyler knew. Sympathy—or worse, pity—clouded his eyes.

A fistful of muscle relaxants couldn't have stopped her spine from stiffening. Granted, Frank would never nominate her for daughter of the year, but now that she was back in Bluelick, she planned on forging some kind of adult relationship with him. In the meantime, she had a pretty good life, if she did say so herself. She set high goals for herself and worked hard to attain them. No pity necessary.

In her haste to close the topic, she replied more brusquely than she intended. "The whole incident serves as a perfect example of what happens when liquor, lame-ass judgment, and dangerous toys come together. Speaking of which"—she cocked an eyebrow at Tyler—"how're you doing this morning?"

Roger cleared his throat and eyed them both speculatively. "I get the distinct impression I'm missing something interesting. Unfortunately, I've got a game with my dad at the club in ten minutes, so I've got to go. Tyler, always a pleasure. Ellie, let's catch up real soon."

See you? Call me? Potential farewells flashed through her mind as he ambled out of the coffee shop, but before she could settle on one, Tyler draped an arm around her shoulders and whispered in her ear.

"I'm doing fine, and so is my lame ass. Thanks for asking."

She shivered and told herself his breath tickling her ear caused the reaction, rather than the unbidden memory of his lips plastered to hers last night during his little "aptitude test." She couldn't deny that the image of his sculpted backside elicited tingles in some highly personal places. Goodness, she felt wilder already. Then again, she'd always been a quick study, particularly when the instructor inspired her interest in the subject. Apparently, Tyler inspired.

Unsure of her next move, she fell back on manners. "I noticed the garbage fairy cleaned up my porch. You didn't have to do that. You're supposed to be taking it easy."

He shrugged. "I made the mess. Least I could do was clean up after myself." His low voice tickled her ear.

"Well...thanks," she managed, around her suddenly dry throat. Her discomfort only intensified when a familiar voice called, "Ellie! I've been hoping to run into you ever since I heard you were back."

Chapter Three

Ellie spun and came face-to-face with Roger's ex-fiancée.

"Oh my gosh, Melody, hi!" Inwardly, she grimaced at the brittle enthusiasm of her reply. "You look beautiful, as always." That much, at least, was true. Her sea-blue sundress matched her eyes and displayed her enviable figure to perfection.

The blonde smiled. "Thanks. So do you. Love your outfit. I wish I could wear cargos, but they make my hips look huge. Hey, Tyler."

"Hey." He flashed a smile and glanced at his watch. "Much as I hate to greet and run, I've got a meeting. Catch you later, Mel. Doc." He leaned in, tucked a flyaway hair behind her ear, and brushed his lips over her cheek. To anyone in the coffee shop, the gesture probably looked exactly the same as Roger's—friendly and innocent. In truth, the kisses were worlds apart. Tyler's kiss stirred up all kinds of reactions, none of which she'd call "friendly" or "innocent." She backed up, still reeling a bit, and he snagged a finger into the vee of her T-shirt to halt her retreat. "See you Thursday," he whispered.

Before she could so much as nod in reply, he shot her a cocky grin and headed out into the sun-soaked morning. She found herself staring after him, admiring how he filled out his Levi's.

"Ellie, I've been wanting to ask you something. Do you have a minute to talk?"

Melody's hesitant tone pulled Ellie's head out of Tyler's pants. During school, gorgeous, popular Melody had rarely sounded unsure. But she did now, and looked it, too, with her questioning eyes and the serious set to her mouth. Whatever she wanted to discuss, the topic clearly made her nervous, and this triggered a domino effect in Ellie.

"Um, sure. Want to walk over to my office with me? It's just on the other side of the square."

Melody nodded. "Perfect."

Yeah, perfect, she thought as they started across Main. The perfect opportunity for Melody to say, "I saw you eavesdropping at DeShay's yesterday and you should mind your own damn business." Braced for anything, she nearly tripped over her feet when Melody said, "I heard you were opening your practice and I wondered if you needed an office manager."

She blinked and tried to get her brain to switch gears. "I called an agency in Lexington and asked them to send a temp on Monday, but I'd love to hire locally, if possible. Why? Do you know someone who might be interested?"

The blonde's tinkling laughter followed them along the pretty row of nineteenth-century brick storefronts. "You could say that."

Ellie stopped in front of the carved limestone steps leading to her office and glanced up at Melody.

"It's me, Ellie. I'm interested."

"But...I thought you worked at Reynolds & Reynolds?"

"Yes, but I'm overdue for a change. I can't work for Roger

Sr. the rest of my life. The grand plan, of course, was for Roger to take over his dad's practice. I'd run the office until we started having kids." She sighed and shrugged. "You've probably heard by now Roger and I broke up, so that's not going to happen. It's time for a new plan. I want...no, I *need* a change."

Melody's words resonated with Ellie. Fate sometimes dealt out disappointments. A healthy person took time to grieve, and then did her best to adapt and overcome. She couldn't blame Melody for not wanting to continue at Reynolds & Reynolds, surrounded by constant reminders that her grand plan hadn't quite panned out.

Some people never moved on. When a three-car pileup on the Double A had robbed Ellie's father of his beloved wife, he'd clung to his pain like a keepsake. She'd watched him grow bitter and resentful, incapable of appreciating his blessings, including her, to the extent that he'd ever been inclined to count her among them.

All the more reason to admire Melody for choosing to move forward, but hiring Roger's ex probably wasn't a good idea.

"I understand, Melody, better than you know. The thing is, I...ah...I like Roger."

"Of course you do. Everyone likes Roger. *I* like Roger. Heck, I love Roger, just not the way you need to love someone you're going to marry. And he feels the same way. Our breakup truly was mutual. We parted friends, so don't worry. You won't get pressed into taking sides."

Ellie stared at the cheerful red geraniums overflowing the window boxes and debated her conscience. What could she say? "I don't just like Roger, I *like* like him." God, no. Too adolescent.

Instead, for some inconceivable reason, she blurted, "Roger told me the breakup was his fault," and immediately wished she could kick herself for bringing up personal details she wasn't entitled to and really didn't want.

"Well, he'd put it that way. Fault's a strong word. We just weren't meant to be. It's fine, Ellie. Really. If you hire me, I don't expect Roger to be dead to you."

"Are you sure you want to work for a start-up doctor still trying to build her practice? The pay probably sucks compared to what you're used to, or could earn in a bigger market like Lexington."

"I like the idea of working in town. There's no quality of life in a long commute. As for the money, tell me, are you a good doctor?"

She thought about her years in medical school, her internship, her residency. She also thought about the neat, precise line of stitches in Tyler's butt. "Yes, I think so."

"Great. I'm a good office manager. So if you do your job, and I do mine, your practice will succeed, and I'm sure the money thing will work out. Right now my goal is to land the job and be useful. Come on. What do you say?"

What could she say? "I'll see you Monday morning, 9:00 a.m.?"

Melody's squeal and fast, firm hug turned heads of passersby along the sidewalk. "Yay! You won't be sorry," she promised as she practically skipped down Main.

"Yeah," Ellie said under her breath. "Hopefully you won't be either."

. . .

Tyler sat in an uninspired gray cubicle at Bluelick Savings and Loan and tried to keep his temper on a leash. "What do you mean you're declining my loan? Did something about my proposal throw you?"

The mountain of flesh known as Grady Landry puffed

out a breath and ran a pudgy hand through his thinning red hair. "Your proposal was clear, and the lending committee acknowledged that a construction loan on a spec property falls within our charter. But part of this institution's mandate is a little something called 'Know your customer,' and you, my friend, are a known risk."

Tyler narrowed his eyes and stared across the desk. Grady wasn't a bad guy, he reminded himself. The man had gone to bat for him five years ago when he'd sought a loan to get his fledgling construction company off the ground. But that made it all the harder to understand why one paid-in-full loan later, they turned him down for another.

"My track record with this institution says different," he said. "The Browning property has been rotting on its foundation for the last twenty years. My team and I can turn that dilapidated old horse farm into a showplace. I'm not talking about razing the buildings, subdividing the acreage, and putting up a bunch of cookie-cutter McMansions for refugees from New York and Philly looking to indulge their horsey fantasies. I'd restore the main house and the barns, and sell the property as the equestrian estate it was meant to be, for three times the loan amount—and you damn well know it. So, sorry, I don't see the risk you're all hung up on."

Grady drummed his fingers on his desk. "I'll sketch it out for you. Let's say we lend you the money you're asking for—a significantly larger amount than your original loan, I should point out—and then something happens to you. How do we make good on our loan? A mortgage on the unimproved property won't do the trick. As far as we can see, nobody on your crew can step in and take your place, so your big plans for the Browning farm go bye-bye. Without you, your company isn't worth close to the loan amount, so liquidating your business assets wouldn't make us whole." He shrugged and held his hands up. "Everybody here likes you and believes in your skills, but I can't sell this to our lending committee because you're the single point of success—or failure."

"I'm thirty-two years old, for God's sake. Neither foot is anywhere near the grave. Do I have to pass a physical or—"

"You ride around on a Harley."

Hell, he knew where this was headed. Still, he'd go down swinging. "I've never had an accident."

"You practically own a barstool at Rawley's."

"C'mon Grady, I see you there often enough."

"I'm not looking for a loan. And I've never found myself on the wrong end of Junior Tillman's small-game rifle at last call. The way my lending committee sees it, you're an accident waiting to happen."

Shit. "Does everybody and their dog know about the thing with Junior?"

The big man nodded. "'Fraid so. The grapevine sprang a few new sprouts over that one. Look Tyler, I want to help, swear to God I do, but you've got to show my lending committee you're stable and responsible."

"Hell." Tyler tossed his paperwork on the desk. "I run an honest business, keep it solidly in the black. I can restore an antebellum horse farm better than anybody south of the Mason-Dixon line. What else do they want?"

"Settle down with a nice girl. Trade the Harley for a minivan and the late nights at Rawley's for parent-teacher conferences. Look like you've got a stake in this life beyond having a good time."

The rough, unvarnished truth hurt. People considered him a hell-raiser who couldn't handle real responsibility. Never mind that he'd founded a business and busted his ass to make it successful. Never mind that he and his team consistently turned out top-notch projects, on time and within budget. His "don't give a damn" image—fairly earned, he hated to admit—stood firmly in the way of his goals.

Tyler stared at the bland tile ceiling and sighed. "A nice girl, a minivan, and parent-teacher conferences, huh? Sounds like a great ten-year plan. Too bad I wanted the loan sometime this decade." He stood and gathered his papers. "Thanks for the honesty, if nothing else."

"Wait," Grady said when Tyler started to walk away. "Wait a week or so for the incident with Junior to blow over. In the meantime, keep the Harley on the back roads and the wild times to a minimum, and come up with a succession plan for Thoroughbred Construction. I don't need an heir apparent, just some information about the management structure and who does what in your operation so my lending committee can understand they're not investing in a one-man show, okay? Do those things and I'll take your application to the committee again."

Tyler swallowed and held out his hand. "Thanks, Grady."

"Save your thanks 'til the loan's approved."

• • •

Forty minutes later, in the foreman's trailer at the Lexington job site, Tyler watched Junior pace and sweat. "Jesus, Ty, I'm sorry about this whole mess. I know you weren't hitting on Lou Ann. I mean, I didn't know it at the time, 'cause I wasn't exactly thinking straight, but once I sobered up, I knew you wouldn't do something like that. Want me to go to Grady and explain?"

"Thanks, Junior, but no. Explanations won't undo the lending committee's impression of me as bad risk. I've got to show them that Thoroughbred Construction is a safe investment."

His friend flopped down on the small sofa along one wall of the trailer, adjusted his ball cap out of habit, and looked up at Tyler with beagle eyes. "I don't know how to repay you for not going to the cops, and convincing the pretty little doc not to call them either. If there's anything I can do to— "

"Get rid of the gun."

"Done. I gave it to Grandpa."

"Good choice." Nobody ever accused the elder Tillman of being irresponsible. Junior's grandparents had stepped in to raise their only grandchild while Junior's parents had run around town like a couple of footloose twenty-somethings— exactly what they'd been in those days. Grandma and Grandpa Tillman never had a lot of money, but they'd always found a spot at the dinner table and a warm bed for Tyler whenever Junior had dragged him home, and had never made him feel like an unwanted stray.

"I know. I'll have to pass a sobriety test and a gun safety quiz before Grandpa lets me so much as oil the damn thing. But what I really meant was what can I do to help you get the loan?"

"Funny you should ask. The bank wants an assurance that Thoroughbred Construction won't go belly-up if I meet an untimely demise. You're going to help me show them my business has a life of its own."

Junior sat up a little straighter. "I am?"

"Yep. Effective immediately, you're the assistant manager of Thoroughbred Construction. You'll see a bump in your next paycheck to reflect the new title."

"Me?"

"Yeah, you. You know the ropes from initial bid through final punch list. You know the crew, the inspectors, who to call when a permit snags."

"Well, sure, show me some plans, point me to the job site, say 'build,' and by God I'll build it. But I'm no businessman. I don't have a clue how to talk to clients, or, you know... lenders."

"You're going to learn, starting now." Tyler pulled the

loan application from his computer bag and tossed it to Junior. "We're meeting with the Bluelick Savings and Loan lending committee in soon, to show them the depth of our management talent. Get familiar with the information in that application."

Junior squinted at the stack of paper and then lifted the cover sheet as if he suspected a snake lurked beneath. For a moment he stared at the glossy cover sheet fronting the package, then scratched the back of his neck and looked up at Tyler. "Oh, buddy, you got the wrong guy. I'm no good with the dog-and-pony stuff. I can't talk fast enough to convince anybody of anything."

"Not true. You convinced me not to call the cops on you last Friday night."

"Oh yeah. There was that." Hunching his shoulders against the weight of the debt, Junior sighed and turned his attention back to the loan documents. "Speaking of fast talking, how'd you get Ellie to keep quiet?"

Tyler shook his head. "You wouldn't believe me if I told you."

Chapter Four

Ellie tugged the last stitch free and ran the pad of her thumb down the slightly raised seam of the healing wound. Even under the bright, florescent exam room light, she could barely see where the stitches had been. "This is healing beautifully. You'll only have a faint scar." She resisted a completely unprofessional urge to run her hand over his entire butt. There was absolutely no medically valid reason for a tactile exam of his glutes.

"That's a big relief, Doc," Tyler drawled. "I'm real vain about that cheek."

She rolled her stool back a couple feet to signal she was done. "Well then, you might try keeping it out of Junior's line of fire."

"That's my plan." He buttoned his jeans, then turned to face her and leaned back against the exam table. "Thanks for fitting me in so late in the day."

"No problem." Goodness, he was tall. True, at five-three, almost everybody topped her, but Tyler towered over her. Plus, he had those wide shoulders, and…was it her imagination, or did the exam room suddenly seem claustrophobically tiny? She stood and backed to the other side, where his chart lay on the top of a stainless steel cabinet. "I know you wanted to keep this little incident on the down-low, so having you come by after Melody left for the day struck me as a good idea."

"That was nice of you, hiring Melody. I'm sure she can use the change of scenery about now."

"Actually, she's the nice one. I'm getting an organized, detail-oriented office manager for a fraction of what an established practice would pay her. I'm, like, her charity project."

"Okay, see how you turned my praise around and aimed it at Melody? That's nice. Add it to kindly digging a bullet out of my ass at two in the morning and not calling the cops on Junior. I don't know"—he aimed his sexy smile at her—"you may have to face the fact that you're a nice person."

"We came to an arrangement on the not calling the cops thing."

"Gonna hold me to that, are you?"

She couldn't guess whether he was teasing her or looking to back out. Defeated by his inscrutability, she exhaled and admitted, "No. I'm not. What I said Friday night still stands. If you're not into this, let's forget the whole deal."

The sexy smile shifted into the bad-boy grin she remembered from years ago. "Oh, I'm into it. Don't you worry."

She scribbled a note in his chart and told her pulse to stop fluttering. Before she could respond, his expression sobered. "I am grateful to you, though. Thank you for taking care of me and being discreet. Junior also sends his thanks and apologies. He wanted me to tell you he gave his gun to his granddad. Figured he didn't need to be driving around with a firearm handy."

"You're welcome. I'm glad Junior got rid of the gun."

"Me, too. So"—he inclined his head toward the chart—"am I cleared for class?"

Restless butterflies fluttered in her stomach. She glanced at him from under her lashes. "Yes."

Two Longfoot strides brought them toe to toe. He simply stared at her for a moment, then raised his hand and swept her hair behind her shoulder. "All right, then. A deal's a deal. Lesson one, Friday at seven. I'll come to you."

She swallowed, nearly choking on her own spit when his strong, capable fingers unerringly found the tight muscles at the base of her neck and began kneading. Reminding herself this was her idea, she nodded. "Okay. I'll figure out the lesson plan."

"You do that, Doc. In the meantime…pop quiz."

"Huh—" That's as far as she got before Tyler's mouth settled on hers. Such a small contact, but once again, it generated instant, addictive heat. She gasped when his tongue traced the sensitive curve of her upper lip. The move melted her bones. She leaned into his strong, warm body for support. His hands cruised up her back, and the calm, logical voice deep inside her mind clicked off. *"Yes!"* flashed behind her eyelids in big, neon letters.

With no oversight whatsoever from her brain, her hands dove into his hair and held on, held his amazing, devastating mouth still on hers. A low, needy cry echoed from somewhere in the tile-and-steel exam room. Belatedly, she realized the inarticulate plea emanated from her.

Apparently Tyler understood, because he cupped the back of her head in his big hand and sent his tongue on a deluxe tour of her mouth. Each touch, slide, or deep, penetrating exploration shot staggering sensations to every pulse point in her body. Those unsuspecting destinations sat up and took notice. Her nipples contracted and her bra suddenly felt way too small for her nowhere-close-to-double-D breasts.

Tension coiled low in her abdomen. She fought the urge to rub her thighs together to relieve the pressure building there.

Somehow, miraculously, he knew about the pressure. He slid one big, muscular thigh between hers, grabbed her backside, and hauled her against him. She practically whimpered with gratitude.

"Hey, Ellie, have you seen my...whoops!" Melody's voice reverberated in the silence.

Ellie broke away, shaken to the core by the unexpected interruption and her reaction to his kiss. No kisses had swept her away like Tyler's. Ever. Had he felt the same intense... heck, she didn't know what to call it...jolt of awareness, sensory recognition, bone-deep *need*?

Hard to say. His expression revealed only lazy amusement as he loosened his hold and let her slide slowly down his body, releasing her a few beats after her feet met the floor. Something mischievous flickered in his eyes and she immediately marched herself into a mental cold shower.

"I'm so sorry," Melody said, sounding more intrigued than apologetic. "I didn't realize you had company."

"No problem, Mel," Tyler replied, completely unfazed. "I was just heading out. See you Friday, Ellie." With a final, unnervingly knowing look, he walked out of the exam room.

Melody managed to hold her tongue until the main door closed, but not a second more. "Why, Sparky Swann!"

"What?" Ellie smoothed her hair and tried to act unruffled, but damp panties and perky nipples didn't do much for her acting abilities. Her body reacted to his skill— nothing more. Researchers could probably explain how the combination of thick black hair, riveting green eyes, and a slow, confident smile provoked some cascade of estrogen designed to fool the female mind into confusing a simple kiss with a merging of souls.

"What do you mean, *what*? You're not back in Bluelick

a month and I find you making out after hours with big, bad Tyler Longfoot." She folded her arms across her chest. "How long has this been going on?"

"Is it hot in here?" Ellie fiddled with the neckline of her blue-and-white-striped top, and then, still stalling, brushed her palms over her white linen pants. "There's nothing going on. It's not what you think. He's just..." Lord, how was she supposed to explain this? "He's assisting me with a personal project."

Melody grinned. "Uh-huh, right. You couldn't find your tonsils so he stopped by to help you look for them. Search to be continued this Friday. If you want my advice, you should have him hunt for something really important, like your G-spot."

"Ha ha." Melody's teasing struck a little too close to home. "Somehow, during all the years we spent as classmates, I never noticed your smart mouth before."

"You were blinded by my good looks. But don't worry, Ellie." Melody's playful smile straightened. "I know how to keep things to myself. As far as I'm concerned, people's personal lives are theirs to advertise or keep in confidence as they see fit. Nobody's going to hear a word about you and Tyler from me."

Determined to downplay the episode, Ellie scooted past Melody. "That's a relief, considering there's nothing to tell."

"Oh, now, I don't know about that. What I saw just saw between you and Tyler looked like a whole lot more than *nothing*."

Chapter Five

Ellie looked around her bedroom and mentally reviewed her checklist. Clean sheets? Check. Condoms? Check. Five chapters carefully flagged in her fully illustrated copy of *The Wild Woman's Guide to Sex: Tactics Guaranteed to Bring a Man to His Knees*? Check. Having studied the guide immediately upon its arrival—via rush delivery, in all its plain, brown-wrapped glory—she'd already employed one of the tactics. She turned to view her reflection in the oval mirror atop her antique oak dresser, slipped out of her robe, and took a detached inventory of the woman staring back at her, dressed for "action."

A black satin-and-lace bra boosted her normally unremarkable cleavage to almost opulent proportions. The imported lace teased her nipples to points with every subtle shift of fabric. It was, quite possibly, the most uncomfortable garment she'd ever worn. No, wait...her gaze dropped. That honor belonged to the matching thong.

Hands on hips, she pivoted to check the rear view. The line of satin dividing her derriere looked to be in the proper place, and there was really only one reasonable path for it to take, but it felt like a wedgie waiting to happen.

Pivoting again, she faced the mirror. The guide advised aspiring wild women to make their peace with the push-up bra and butt floss because…ta-da…the combination brought men to their knees.

She shrugged on her robe and tied the belt. She didn't care about all men, just Roger. He was definitely worth the discomfort. Besides, she didn't have the natural advantages of a Melody Merritt or a Lou Ann Doubletree. She needed all the help she could get.

Thankfully, a big dose of "help" was due any moment in the form of Tyler Longfoot. The sound of a motorcycle approaching confirmed the thought, and caused a winged migration from her chest to her stomach. She grabbed a tube of gloss from the dresser and retouched her lips with an unsteady hand.

Why so nervous? Was she afraid he'd laugh at her attempt to be sexy? Maybe…okay, yes. Silly, because while she really didn't know him very well, she knew he wouldn't deliberately hurt her feelings. The real worry was that they'd get into what she'd selected as the first lesson and he'd deem her a hopeless case.

Unlikely, she reassured herself, because she'd studied chapter 3 diligently. The guide claimed most men loved chapter 3 anytime, anywhere, with any degree of proficiency, so it made a fairly foolproof starting point. Hopefully. Maybe it was too conventional? Should she have started with chapter 13?

The chime of her doorbell ended her second-guessing. She rushed to the door, pulled it open, and stopped short. For whatever reason, she'd assumed he'd come directly from his job site, and had pictured him in work boots and dusty jeans. Instead he stood before her freshly showered and smooth-jawed, with a devilish gleam in his clear, green eyes. The clean, spicy scent of his aftershave enticed her almost as much as the rest of him.

"Oh, good, you're here. Right on time. That's helpful, because we have a lot to cover this evening." Since she couldn't seem to stop babbling, she gestured him in. "We should probably get started. My bedroom's this way." She laughed a little hysterically. "Of course you don't need me to tell you. You already know the layout."

"Whoa. Slow down, there, Sparky." He snagged her arm and, with a tug, brought her swinging around until her chest bumped his.

Her heart thudded against her ribs. She took a step back and tried to figure out what she'd rushed. "I'm sorry. Did you want to…" What? What did guys like to do before getting it on? "Freshen up, or, was there something else you needed?"

His slow smile tightened her stomach. "Maybe I need a little wine and candlelight first, hmm?" Fingers toyed with the ends of her hair. "I'm not a windup toy, you know."

He was teasing her, she felt certain, but still, she could be a good hostess. "Um, I have some chardonnay in the fridge, if you'd like a glass. Could we put the candlelight off until next week? I need to see what I'm doing for this first lesson—"

His laugh cut her off, deep and rich and completely without taunt, but her hackles rose anyway. Here she was, organized, prepared, ready to get to work, and he was messing around.

"I actually wasn't making a joke."

Her outburst bounced off him. He trailed his fingers down her arm as if he enjoyed the feel of her skin. "I'm sure you weren't. Look, Doc, I worked a long day, came home, showered, and got myself over here. I need sustenance."

Sustenance? "You're hungry?"

"Aren't you?"

She opened her mouth to say no, but her stomach rumbled.

His smile deepened. "C'mon, Ellie, get dressed. It's a pretty evening. Let's take a ride over to the river and grab some dinner. There's nothing wild about one of us passing out from hunger."

"B-but I'm already prepared here. I've got fancy underwear on and everything."

He cocked one dark eyebrow. "That so?" Big hands took her shoulders and turned her around. His mouth moved next to her ear. "I can't wait to hear all about them over dinner. Go throw on a little dress and a jacket. I'll wait in the front room." One hand slid down her back, over her butt, and squeezed.

"Tyler— "

"Hurry." He gave her backside a playful swat and nudged her toward her bedroom.

• • •

When Ellie strode into her front room, Tyler rose from her dainty blue sofa and all the blood in his head flowed due south at record speed.

The deep purple dress she'd changed into hugged her tightly on top and dipped low enough in front to give him a mouthwatering glimpse of cleavage. The short, fluttery skirt showed off a lot of leg—slim, silky legs he instantly pictured wrapped around his waist while the pointed heels on her mile-high sandals dug into his ass like spurs.

"Nice," he managed to say, and helped her into her thin black cardigan.

"Thanks," she said, sounding a little out of breath. "I'm ready."

"After you."

The high-heeled sandals forced her to take her time, so he occupied himself checking out her legs while she preceded him down the porch steps. When she walked toward her garage he caught her arm.

"I'll drive."

She eyed his bike, then him. "You're joking, right?"

"What's the matter, Doc? Scared to ride with me?"

Her expression said, *Hell yes.* "I did an ER rotation during my residency. I saw a lot of rides that didn't turn out as planned."

"Past time you learned how a ride should go. Ours will be short and easy. You'll love it. Trust me." Not wanting to give her an opening to argue, he turned and straddled the big machine. Then he looked back and handed her the helmet. She hesitated.

"Come on, Doc. You're the one who wants to be more adventurous between the sheets. Step one—be more adventurous out of them. If you can't handle a sunset ride down a country road on a warm June night"—he shrugged—"might as well call Magnolia Grove and see if they've got a villa for you."

"Magnolia Grove?"

"It's a retirement community about halfway between here and Lexington. Very safe and peaceful, although I hear they've got extreme bingo if you think you can handle it."

His taunt did the trick. She shoved the helmet over her head and stared him down. "How do I get on this blasted thing?"

It took three tries, and he got a very nice sneak peek at her new underwear in the process, but finally she sat behind him, her slim thighs around his hips, her front pressed against his back. The slope of the seat didn't allow for any other position. Instant intimacy.

"You're going to want to hold on." He took her hands

and wrapped her arms around his waist, biting back a smile when she laced her fingers together in a white-knuckled grip. "Ready?"

"Um, okay," came her reluctant reply.

Good enough. He brought his right foot down hard on the kick-start lever and cranked the accelerator. The machine revved to life, but not quite in time to drown out her squeal. She clung to him as they rocketed down her driveway.

• • •

The purr of the engine obliterated any other noise she might have made, but it couldn't hide the way her arms tightened to a death grip and her fingernails dug into his stomach. As a rule, he liked having a date pressed up against him so close a sheet of paper couldn't squeeze between them, and so distracted by what he was doing to her that she put a few scratches on him. But he preferred to inspire that kind of mindless urgency during a slightly different activity. He settled a hand over hers and gave a squeeze. It seemed to help, a little.

Not that he didn't get the reason for her anxiety. He did. Neither of them had been raised to trust easily, and hurtling down the open road with nothing but his skill standing between her and an up-close, personal encounter with the asphalt required a fair amount of trust. That understanding made it all the sweeter when, after a mile or so, her grip loosened infinitesimally and her body relaxed against his. Some natural instinct kicked in and she started to flow with the movement of the bike, and him. Tension he'd barely registered drained out of his neck and shoulders. Better. Much better. Now they could both sit back and enjoy the ride—the warm wind, the smell of honeysuckle in the air, the sinking sun bathing everything in orange and gold.

Those relatively innocent pleasures weren't the only ones

to enjoy. Every time he leaned into one of the meandering turns, she leaned into him. Her arms tightened around his waist and the hard, hot points of her nipples drilled into his back. The way she squirmed and clenched her thighs when he accelerated told him she felt the vibrations of the bike's powerful engine in all the right places.

By the time the tin roof and weathered planks of The Catch came into view, she'd melted against him like a cheddar square on a hot slice of pie. He pulled into the restaurant's busy parking lot, cut the engine, and heard her small, breathy sigh. Oh yeah, she liked the ride.

Bracing the bike with one leg, he slid his hand along her thigh. "You good with this, Doc?"

She pulled the helmet off. In his side mirror, he watched her give him a long, wary look, as if she might not be so sure about their bargain. He found himself holding his breath.

Then she nodded. "Absolutely, I'm good with this." Chin raised, she smiled at him.

"Great. Better grab on."

"Wha— ?" The word ended in a high note as he hefted the bike onto its kickstand. Her hands clutched his shoulders.

He waited while she got off the bike. As far as he could judge from his limited perspective, her underwear didn't make an encore appearance during her dismount, but letting her use his body like a ladder to climb down stirred up his imagination almost as well. She wobbled a little when she stepped back to give him room. He pushed off the bike, closed the distance, and wrapped his arm around her waist. "That wasn't so bad, was it?"

"No," she said, sounding a bit startled by the admission. More pleased than he expected to be by one little word, he steered her along the short pier to the restaurant's entrance.

He opened the door for her and followed her through, accidentally bumping into her when she stopped abruptly.

He caught her arms to steady her when the impact knocked her off-balance, and then, for no reason except she smelled incredible and felt so damn good, he turned her to face him and very slowly, very deliberately pulled her in close until his chest brushed her breasts. She looked up at him with an expression somewhere between flustered and exasperated. He flashed his best innocent smile, not missing the pulse pounding away at the base of her throat. *Ride's not over yet, Sparky.*

"Hungry?"

"Yes." The word came out like a confession and he suspected she wasn't referring to food. "But this place is pretty crowded. We might have a long wait."

"They'll have a table for us." Taking her hand, he led her through the press of bodies.

Diane, the manager, spotted him before they made it to the hostess desk and wrapped him in a big hug. "Hey, sugar! I didn't know you were coming in tonight." She eased back, slid a curious glance toward Ellie, and raised a brow at him. "Table for two?"

"Can you squeeze us in?"

She laughed and smoothed a hand over her strawberry-blond hair. "Oh, sugar, I can always squeeze *you* in. And your friend."

"Ellie," he added, sliding his arm around her. "Ellie, Diane."

"Nice to meet you," Ellie said.

"Always nice to meet one of Tyler's friends," Diane returned. "We just love him around here. C'mon." Taking a couple menus from the hostess station, she led them to a quiet corner table on the outdoor dining deck floating above the Ohio River.

Once they were seated, Diane wished them a "memorable" evening, winked at Ellie and departed. The steady slap of water against the deck pilings filled the silence.

"She seems nice," Ellie finally said, absently pushing the small votive candle around on the white linen tablecloth. The low light on the deck turned her brown eyes into deep pools he could get lost in.

"Diane? She is nice. I've known her a long time." He could spend some serious time on Ellie's mouth, too.

"Is 'known her a long time' a euphemism for 'dated her'?" The question startled him out of his distraction with Ellie's lips. Before he could answer, she winced. "Sorry, erase the question. Who you've dated is none of my business. New topic—"

"She's a friend. I got to know her when I remodeled the first restaurant she managed." He couldn't say why her question—and her obvious discomfort about asking—stirred him up, but it did. It also renewed his curiosity about her underlying reason for the whole "sex tutor" deal. "Anything else you want to know?"

She shook her head and opened her menu. "Nope. I'm good."

"Because unlike some people, *I'm* an open book."

She shut the menu. "And I'm not?"

Just then a waiter appeared and took their drink orders. When he left, Ellie crossed her arms, leaned back in her chair, and stared at him.

He stared right back, issuing a not-so-subtle challenge.

She blinked first and lowered her eyes. "How long have you had the bike?"

"Now we're really getting personal. A long time." Shrugging off a vague disappointment, he added. "Maybe too long."

"Is there a statute of limitations on riding a motorcycle?"

"I'm learning yes, to some folks. But that's a story for another time. Ever been here before?"

"No, never, but this is nice." She stared out at the lights twinkling along the opposite bank of the river and breathed deeply. "Before I left for college, Bluelick's version of fine dining meant Rawley's or the place off the Double A with the statue of the husky kid in red-checked overalls."

He laughed. "I save the kid in the overalls for the second date."

"This isn't really a date."

"Says who? I see you, single, attractive female. Me, single, available guy. Moonlight and candles. What more do you need before you call it a date?"

"We have an arrangement," she replied primly, and straightened in her chair, which only made him want to kiss her senseless.

"Wasn't aware they were mutually exclusive. Maybe you should tell me what you're really trying to accomplish with our arrangement."

"I've already told you. New topic."

"Ellie."

"New topic," she repeated. "How long has The Catch been here? I don't remember anything except run-down old buildings."

He held his response until the waiter served their drinks, then took a swallow of his iced tea before continuing. "About three years. My team did the renovations on this building, which were substantial considering we started with a neglected, century-old tobacco warehouse. We managed to rehab about sixty percent of the original structure."

She looked around again. "Wow. You worked a miracle. The walls whisper with history, but at the same time, it's comfortable and relaxed...and the view. I can understand why it's such a popular spot."

"Pretty view, plus they serve up the best shrimp and ribs you ever tasted."

The waiter returned and asked if they were ready to order.

Tyler arched a brow at her. She nodded. "I hear the shrimp is excellent."

"Shrimp *and* ribs," he corrected, and pointed to a nearby table where a server delivered plates piled high with skewers of barbecue shrimp and racks of baby back ribs. "Surf and turf, Bluelick style."

Her gorgeous mouth fell open. "Oh my God. I can't eat that much."

"You were hungry when I picked you up. You must be downright starving after our ride."

Her eyes cut to his and she shifted in her seat. The tiny move told him she remembered every aspect of their ride, in intimate detail. *He* remembered the flash of black silk beneath her skirt. Continuing in a deliberately seductive drawl, he said, "I want to make sure we completely satisfy your appetite."

The waiter coughed and cleared his throat. "Two shrimp and ribs?"

Tyler nodded. The young man smiled politely and departed.

Ellie squirmed again and then glanced at Tyler.

He leaned in, close enough to smell her perfume. "Tell me, Doc, how's the underwear working out for you?"

She twirled the stem of her wineglass between restless fingers and stared out at the river. "They're very, um, distracting."

"I think that's part of the thrill. If it's any consolation, they've been distracting me ever since you mentioned them."

The soft light played over the curve of her cheek and wove midnight highlights in the dark curtain of her hair. He gave in to the urge to sweep it back from her face, so he could see her eyes.

"I have to say, I'm flattered you dressed up for me, so to speak."

"Well, I'm no Lou Ann. I need all the enhancements."

He scooted his chair closer. She jerked in surprise when he slid his hand under the tablecloth and over her knees. "You do not," he said softly.

She resorted to quoting the authorities. "The book I ordered included very specific information about the proper attire for this kind of thing."

"The book?" Determined to prove her wrong, he insinuated his hand between her knees.

"What are you doing?" Her voice came out slightly pitchy.

"Making a point." He eased his hand under her knee and ran it slowly along her calf, lifting her leg in the process. "You're expanding your horizons, remember? Answer the question. What book?"

"I ordered a how-to guide so I could figure out what I needed to learn and, you know..." She trailed off when he curled his fingers around her delicate ankle and removed her strappy high-heeled sandal. "...study, so I'd be prepared."

"Let me get this straight. You decide you want more action and adventure in your sex life, so first thing you do is buy a book and study up? Does that strike you as ironic?" He ran his thumb slowly along her arch, applying just enough pressure to make her moan.

"It's...logical," she finally managed.

"Logical, huh?" *Keep a straight face*, he ordered himself, but his lips twitched.

"Jeez, Tyler, don't hurt yourself. Go ahead and laugh, but I honestly don't see what's so funny. If I want to improve at something, I learn as much as I can about the topic and then put what I've learned into practice. Why approach this any differently?"

Her irritation, as much as her linear reasoning, unleashed

the laugh he'd struggled to hold back. She tried to tug her foot free, but he held on.

"Simmer down, Doc. I'm about to show you why." With that, he placed her foot in the V between his legs, so there was no way she could miss the highly compelling evidence supporting his argument. "You do this to me just the way you are. No fancy underwear or how-to book needed."

Her eyes widened, and then, yes, there it was. She blushed.

"I'm sure it's just the wine and candlelight. Or tea and candlelight, in your case." Although she tried to joke, her toes curled into him, torturing him with the small exploration.

He wrapped his hand around the top of her foot, holding here there. "It's not the candlelight." He squeezed her foot and swept his thumb over her ankle. "I'd love to know why it's so tough to believe you alone might do the job. Why you think you need lessons on driving a man wild? Enlighten me, Doc."

Chapter Six

Ellie wasn't sure she could speak to reply. Tyler kept one hand on her foot, nestling it intimately against him, while his other hand journeyed up her calf. Even if she could talk, she had no intention of coming clean. Roger's tastes, and her desire to satisfy them, weren't for public consumption.

"What if I told you this is the raciest dinner I've ever had in my life?" she asked.

"I'd say it's not over yet." As proof, his nimble fingers rounded the curve of her knee and continued up her thigh.

She grasped the table and moaned softly as those big, blunt fingers stroked dangerously close to the thin strip of silk providing a flimsy barrier between her and a complete physical meltdown.

"Definitely not over," he said, and stroked again.

"Don't," she groaned, and dropped her hand beneath the table to grip his wrist. But at the same time she scooted closer to the edge of her chair. She was sending mixed messages and couldn't seem to help it.

"Want me to stop?" Even as he posed the question, his

fingers danced a little farther up her thigh. Concentration became impossible. Her pulse skittered out of control, pounding in her throat, her chest, between her legs.

"I think…yes…I think you'd better."

He leaned closer until she drowned in his eyes. "Okay," he whispered, and slowly trailed his hand back down the soft, vulnerable flesh of her thigh. She shivered.

He smiled. "What you're feeling right now? That's exactly how I feel when I look at you. You're as hot as they come, so do me a favor and stop comparing yourself to Lou Ann. Deal?"

God, she felt hot right now, with his eyes locked on hers and her body still quivering from his touch. She also felt stripped bare and defenseless, because he seemed to see straight through to some long-buried insecurities.

Her father hadn't been the type to dispense compliments. To Frank she'd been a duty, a chore, and a painful reminder of the wife he'd lost too soon. The less attention she demanded from him, the better. Teachers gave her positive feedback on her academic performance, and because she'd been starving for praise, she'd focused her efforts there. Which might explain why she could attack any academic pursuit with confidence, but the rest—looks, personality, feminine allure—remained big, fat question marks. She never realized how much she cared about the answers until Tyler volunteered his. Thankfully the waiter's approach saved her the need to formulate an immediate reply.

The server delivered their meals and retreated. She stared at her plate, momentarily distracted by the mountain of food in front of her.

"Deal?" Tyler prompted, holding a shrimp to her lips.

"Deal," she murmured. Lowering her eyes, she closed her mouth around the shrimp, expecting him to release it. Instead he slowly pulled until the curled delicacy sprang free with a soft pop. His playful grin coaxed an answering smile from her.

"Does any woman manage to resist you?"

"Some do. But tonight, I'm inspired."

"Hope you're also hungry, because this is far too much food."

"Don't worry, Doc. I know what I'm doing."

She nibbled a rib and then licked the spicy sauce from her lips. "I'm counting on that."

. . .

On the ride back to Ellie's house, Tyler racked his brain to remember the last time dinner with a woman had been so fascinating, sexy, and plain old fun. She engaged him on levels he didn't expect—like her genuine appreciation for the work he'd done on the restaurant. He enjoyed building, enjoyed constructing something innovative and lasting, but rehabbing and renovating old buildings held special appeal. They were hard jobs to bid, because surprises lurked behind every wall and under every floorboard, yet he loved the challenge and the satisfaction of seeing a slice of history standing tall and proud at the end of the project.

Women's eyes usually glazed over when he mentioned his work, but Ellie had listened with real interest and found parallels between their professions. According to her, he examined, diagnosed, and healed the old structures so they could thrive again. The words made him smile. He'd never thought about what he did in quite those terms, but her assessment got down to the heart of it. Her quick mind and, yes, those elusive dimples captivated him to the point that he'd had to consciously stop himself from unloading the sad story of his ambitions for the Browning project.

Of course, the weight of her breasts crushed against his

back and her legs clenched snugly around his hips engaged him, too, but on a level he completely expected. He still couldn't fathom why she thought she needed to be wilder, more experienced…whatever. But he looked forward to helping her expand her horizons. Maybe he'd been wrong about taking things slow. She seemed pretty certain about what she wanted from him. He still figured she had a hidden agenda, but fine, they weren't soul mates, just bedmates for the next little while. So what if yet another person assumed the bedroom brought out his best talents?

This time when he stopped the bike in her driveway, she leaned into him for balance and slid off with ease. Fast learner. He appreciated how the hem of her little skirt danced high on her thighs as she walked up the front steps. When she pulled the key from her small shoulder bag and tried to fit it in the lock, her hands shook just enough to make the target difficult.

"Shoot," she said under her breath.

He eased up behind her until his chest brushed her shoulder blades. Scents of gardenia and vanilla wafted from her hair, her skin. She smelled pretty and feminine and…edible.

"Problem?"

"No." With her head bent forward, a cascade of wavy dark hair shielded her face from his view. She shoved the key into the lock, twisted the knob, and swore again when the door didn't budge.

Holding back a chuckle, he used a finger to move her hair out of the way and looked at her. "You sure?"

Wide, vexed eyes stared back at him. He covered her hand with his and twisted the doorknob the other way. The lock mechanism released and the door opened. *Reverse course*, he ordered all the blood that had settled between his legs during the ride back to her place. Ellie was about to jump out of her skin, which only reinforced his original instinct to take things slow—way slower than her beloved lesson plan.

She stared at the door like she wanted to kick it, then exhaled and gave him a sheepish look. "Maybe I'm a little nervous." Her eyes shifted away and she rambled on in what he was beginning to recognize as another sign of nerves. "I don't know why. I mean, this whole thing was my idea. I have everything planned out, and I'm as prepared as possible. I've got the bedroom all set up."

God, she really was adorable when she went all type A on him. "Invite me in for a drink, Doc."

"Oh, right. Please come in." She hurried inside and was halfway to the kitchen by the time he shut the door. Then she stopped in her tracks, and turned to him, all pink and flustered. "Would you like chardonnay, or...I'm sorry, I don't have any beer. I received a bottle of Maker's Mark as a housewarming present, if you prefer something harder?"

He was plenty hard already, thank you very much. But she definitely needed to unwind. "Bourbon's fine, as long as I'm not drinking alone."

Now she looked hesitant. "I don't know. I already had a glass of wine with dinner and I'm not much of a drinker. I don't want to get tipsy, because, despite alcohol's entrenchment in the American mating ritual, depressants actually don't do much for female performance. Male either, for that matter." Heading to the kitchen, she added, "I should probably make yours with plenty of ice and water."

Now he did laugh. There he stood, smack in the middle of her hallway with a hard-on like a steel joist in his jeans, and she was worried about him getting it up.

He wandered in to find her reaching into a high cabinet for the bourbon. Going over her head, he retrieved the bottle and placed it on the counter. "Don't water down good bourbon. That's a sacrilege. I don't know about the other guys you've done this with, Doc, but *I'm* not gonna wilt after one drink."

Then a thought slammed into his head like a two-by-four and nearly knocked him off his feet. He took her chin and tipped her face toward his. "Ah, you have done this before, right?"

She frowned. "Of course."

"More than once?"

Drawing herself up—all five feet and a handful of inches—she crossed her arms over her chest and gave him the stern look that, for some twisted reason, made him want to do all kinds of depraved things to her. "Not that it's any of your business, Tyler, but I've had sex plenty of times. I had a boyfriend during med school and another the final year of my residency."

"Well, shit, Sparky. You be the teacher and I'll be the student."

"Ha ha." She took two lowball glasses from another cabinet, added ice, and placed them on the counter.

He poured them each two fingers and capped the bottle. Then he picked up his glass, tapped it to hers, and took a sip. "So, with all this vast prior experience, what makes you think you need tutoring?"

She shrugged, but her eyes evaded his when she replied and he knew he wasn't going to the get whole story. "My relationships were very, um, conventional, I guess. To be honest, sex wasn't a huge priority, compared to classes and rounds. More like a study break—a nice way to relieve stress. But now, I want more. I want to deliver the fireworks and lightning you read about in novels." She turned and stared uncomfortably out the window.

She thought sex was "nice"? Hmm. "These guys you were with, though…they got the job done for you, right?"

Her eyes flicked to his, then skittered away again. "Um, sort of?"

"Sort of? The question requires a yes or no answer, Doc."

"It was hit or miss," she replied briskly, but her tone told him better than words it was mostly miss. She gulped half her drink, slapped a hand to her chest as she swallowed, and added, "That's not really my focus here, Tyler. I need to learn how to fulfill a man's desires."

Well, she had her focus, he had his. "Hit or miss" wasn't his style. He put his drink aside and considered things for a moment. "I think your aim is fundamentally flawed."

She frowned. "Why?"

"In my experience, which might be just a little bit broader than yours, if my partner isn't having at least as much fun as I am, that's kind of a mood killer."

Her frown deepened and he wondered how he kept himself from sinking his teeth into that pouty lower lip. "According to the manual—"

"Let's take a look at this manual of yours."

"Fine." She downed the rest of her drink and placed the empty glass on the counter. "Great, actually, as that gets us back on plan. Follow me."

She wobbled on the turn. He caught her elbow and kept her on course as they made their way to her room. Once there, she walked to the brass bed, sat heavily on the fluffy white duvet, and shrugged out of her cardigan. The room struck him as pure Ellie—unique and unfussy, but unmistakably feminine. She favored light colors and wood accents. Gesturing to her nightstand, she smiled proudly. "I've got everything we need right here."

"And then some," he agreed as he took a seat beside her.

"What do you mean?"

He pointed to the tube of lube. "As long as I have two hands and a tongue, we're not going to need the Astroglide."

She tapped the book on her nightstand. "The guide specifically recommended it."

"Yeah, yeah, the guide. He skimmed the title and noted the five green tags peeking neatly from the side. "May I?"

She nodded and offered it to him. "I guess now would be a good time to let me know if you have any objections. I flagged the chapters I want you to help me with."

"Of course you did." Taking the manual, he quickly flipped through. If he found highlighted text or margin notes, he might have to sweep his good intentions aside and ball her overactive brains out, right then and there. "Let's see…" He opened to the first tab. "Chapter 3, no problem."

"Good."

He flipped the pages to the next flagged chapter. "Chapter 6, fine, but we'll need to go shopping unless you've already got—?"

"No, we'll need to buy the…ah…accoutrements."

"Leave it to a woman to find an excuse to shop for something as basic as sex. I know a place in Lexington—"

"I figured online would be more private and convenient."

He shook his head and tipped the book to the side to take in an illustration. "No. Field trip to Lexington is the way to go. This is the kind of thing where you want to be able to handle the merchandise before you make a purchase."

"Okay," she sighed. "We'll work in a trip to Lexington." Her tone made him smile. He'd messed with her precious plan again.

"Anything else?"

"Don't know yet." He advanced to the next flag. "Chapter 9 is one of my personal favorites…and 10," he added, flipping again. When he came to the tab on chapter 13, however, he paused, reread the title, and then glanced through the text and illustrations to make sure he hadn't misinterpreted anything. Was she serious? A quick glace her way suggested she was. "I'm vetoing this one." With his index finger, he tapped the page.

"Why?"

"Well, first off, you won't like it, and second, in case you had other ideas, I sure as hell don't want you doing it to me."

She took the book from him and read furiously. "Be serious. I'm not even equipped to do it to you. You do it to me. According to the experts, men love chapter 13. See?" She shoved the damn thing in his face, her finger pointing insistently to the five stars preceding the section.

He moved the book aside. "I don't care what the book says. Trust me, your so-called experts don't know everyth—"

"Look, I chose all the five-star items and chapter 13 is one of them. If you don't help me with it, I'll have to find someone who will."

The comment brought an immediate flare of some unfamiliar emotion he refused to name. He battled a strong urge to toss the book out the window, throw her down on the bed, and show her she already knew exactly what to do to bring a man to his knees.

She must have sensed she'd rubbed him the wrong way, because those long lashes lowered, then rose a bit and she looked at him from beneath. "Please?"

Ah, hell. "We'll see," he replied reluctantly, figuring he had a few weeks to get her to lose interest in chapter 13. "I take it you penciled in chapter 3 for our first lesson?"

She nodded. "We should get started." With that romantic lead-in, she reached for his fly. He intercepted. Hell yeah, they were slowing things down. Why she wanted these lessons might still be a mystery, but he'd learned something about himself—namely, a stripped-down, strictly sexual arrangement didn't interest him. Not with her anyway.

"Let's try something else first." Before she could answer, he cupped her jaw and brought his mouth down on hers.

Slow, deep, deliberately thorough, he delved and tasted before pulling back to look at her.

She slowly unveiled those big brown eyes and he noticed her dilated pupils—wide and open and locked on him.

"Chapter 2—'The Ins and Outs of Kissing'?" she

whispered.

Christ, she was too much. "Important to master the fundamentals, don't you think?"

She nodded, so he obliged. This time he skimmed his teeth over her soft lips, grazing the upper, biting her lush, full lower one until she made an urgent little sound deep in her throat. Her fingers sank into his hair and she pulled his mouth down hard on hers. All the simmering tension of the evening came bubbling to the surface, making the kiss rougher, hungrier, than he planned. But she curved her hand around his neck, leaned into him, and gave as good as she got.

Her mouth moved under his, her lips fast and fierce and silently demanding. Tight nipples poked insistently into his chest, driving him insane. He desperately wanted to lower the zipper at the back of her dress, shove it down, and suck those diamond-hard points into his mouth, but if he did, he wouldn't be able to stop until he had her spread out on the bed with her legs wrapped around his neck, chapter 3-ing her until she couldn't see straight. While that might suit her plans to a tee, chapter 3 wasn't on his agenda for tonight. To distract himself, he slid his hands along her throat until his thumbs caressed her collarbones. She clasped her other hand around his neck and arched against him. An unconscious offer every part of him from the neck down wanted to accept—hell, was dying to accept—but his masochistic brain said *no.*

Jumping into bed with her on the first date might be incredibly satisfying on a physical level, but the move wouldn't do much toward proving there was more to him than low morals and high testosterone. Tonight's date doubled his resolve to show them both he had something to offer besides five-star sex.

He kissed her waiting lips one last time, then eased away and said, "I've got to go."

Chapter Seven

"What?" Ellie opened her eyes and stared at Tyler as if he'd lost his mind. "You can't leave now. We haven't tackled chapter 3."

"No worries. We'll get to it next time."

"No, no, no." She pulled away and shot to her feet. "I've scheduled chapter 6 for next time. If we don't do chapter 3 tonight, we'll be a week behind."

He waited her out while she paced and sputtered. Finally, he walked over until they stood toe to toe, cupped the back of her head, and sent his other hand on a slow slide down her back to rest just above the sweet curve of her ass. "Gives us more to look forward to, right?"

"Tyler, this isn't about building anticipation. Please focus on the schedule."

"What's the big hurry, Doc? You need to extend that schedule of yours to include a little more of this." He hauled her against him and crushed his lips down on hers, doing his level best to scramble her schedule-obsessed brain. She held on and moaned while the kiss became a fast, hot duel of lips and tongues.

When he nibbled his way along her jaw, he had the satisfaction of hearing her breath catch in her throat. His lips brushed her earlobe. She shivered. "I really do have to go," he murmured. "I've got a thing in Ashland at the crack of dawn." Technically true, although the commitment had zero to do with why he was leaving tonight, when every cell in his body begged to stay and finish the job.

"Fine," she sighed and wiggled out of his arms. "Don't let me interfere with your duck hunt, or deer hunt, or whatever the heck guys wake up early and drive to some backwoods place like Ashland to do." She plopped down onto her bed and grabbed the book off the nightstand. "I'll rework the schedule. I may want to combine a couple of lessons next time to get us back on track, but tonight doesn't count as one of our five."

"That's some gratitude." He sat beside her, nipped her earlobe, and looked over her shoulder as she leafed through the manual.

"Which of these would make a good double-header? How about we tackle chapters 3 and 13 next Friday?"

How 'bout we knock all five chapters out right now, the part of his brain most directly connected to his dick suggested. It wasn't easy, but he ignored the errant thought. "I vetoed chapter 13, remember?"

"You said, 'We'll see.'"

"'We'll see,' doesn't mean 'next Friday.' Pick something else."

She sent him a perturbed look and, because he'd been pushed beyond his limits over the last few hours, he fantasized about chapter 6-ing the look right off her face.

"Hmm. What about chapter 4? It only gets three stars, but I feel like I ought to master phone sex, sexting, and all the related technologies. Plus, we could work the lessons in at our convenience. No face-to-face required."

No good. He wanted the face-to-face. *Think fast.* "I don't spend much of my day holed up in an office. Half the time I'm taking calls and checking texts, I'm surrounded by a crew of guys. They might be prone to comment if I text you a picture of my junk."

"A privacy issue? Seriously?" Suspicion laced her voice. "Can't you step into a restroom or something?"

"Have you ever *been* to a construction site? I hate to break this to you, but I'm not feeling real sexy when I'm standing in a port-a-potty."

"Okay, okay." She blew out a breath and flipped the page. "No chapter 4. What about chapter 7? I originally ruled it out because of the slip-and-fall risk, but shower sex gets four stars."

His mind instantly filled with images of Ellie in his shower, all sleek and wet and wrapped around him, her cries of ecstasy echoing in his ears while water pounded down on them and he pounded into her. Shit. He needed to get the hell out of here, right now, before his cock voted for him.

Swallowing to combat the desert in his throat, he answered, "Chapter 7 has potential. I'll think about it." He would. Constantly. Until he went batshit crazy.

She nodded, still absorbed in the text. "I could put some of those no-slip strips in the bottom of my shower. I'm sure they sell them at the hardware store."

Not sure whether to laugh or pound his head against the nearest wall, he eased off the bed. "Honey, I've got to go."

She put the book aside and started to stand, but he put his hands on her shoulders to stop her. "No, no, don't get up." If she hugged him, hell, if she pressed herself against him in any way, shape, or form, he was a goner.

Thankfully, she sank back down to the bed. "All right." Polite as a schoolgirl remembering her manners, she added,

"Thank you for dinner."

He laughed and, giving in to impulse, bent down and kissed her—quick and hard—then released her before he got any closer to chucking *his* plan. "Sweet dreams, Sparky. I'll see myself out."

"Don't call me Sparky," she called after him.

• • •

"Hey, Sparky, wait up!"

Ellie winced as her nickname reverberated across the town square, but when she turned to see Roger jogging up, all traces of irritation vanished.

"Hi, Roger." Thank God she'd dressed for the office today, she thought as she ran her hands over her tan pencil skirt. He, on the other hand, looked uncharacteristically... rugged. His normally perfect hair needed a comb and, if her eyes didn't deceive her, contained flecks of sawdust. The high humidity index alone didn't explain his sweat-dampened T-shirt or the wrinkles in his tan cargo shorts. "What on earth have you been up to?"

He looked down at himself and grimaced. "I was over in Ashland all day building a Habitat house."

She shook her head. "A Habitat house?"

"Habitat for Humanity," he explained as he fell in step beside her. "It's a charity dedicated to putting roofs over peoples' heads. I recently began volunteering. My chance to play Bob the Builder for a day."

Could he be more perfect? Handsome, intelligent, *and* charitable. "That's wonderful, lending your talents to a good cause."

"Well, I don't know about talents. Mostly I'm a strong back and two unskilled hands. But every able body helps. We made a lot of progress today. Unfortunately"—he held out one hand, heel up—"sometimes progress comes at a cost."

She took his smooth, well-manicured hand in hers and examined the splinter wedged into the pad of flesh below his thumb. "Ouch."

"Yeah. Stubborn little bugger. I spent the last half hour going after it with a pair of tweezers, but I think I only worked it in deeper. Then I called Melody, because...well...old habits, I guess, plus I figured she'd enjoy stabbing at me for a while, but she told me you went to the office today and suggested I give you a call. I was about to do that when I spotted you."

Of course he'd call Melody first, she told herself, swallowing disappointment. They'd been a couple forever, and were still close. What mattered was that he sought her out now. He needed her. "Good timing. You just caught me. Let's go upstairs and I'll take care of you."

"Thanks Ellie, I appreciate it." His dazzling smile heated her cheeks.

"No problem." She floated back to her office and led him into an exam room.

While she probed with her tweezers for the end of the splinter, she asked, as casually as possible, "Do you have big plans for your Saturday night?"

"Hmm? Oh. Nothing major. A friend of mine from New York is in Lexington. I'm driving over and meeting him for dinner. We might hit a club or something afterward."

For one fanciful second, she imagined Roger and her as a couple, spending the evening in Lexington with his out-of-town friend. It sounded a million times better than her actual plan— the weekly check-in with Frank. Drop off groceries, test his blood sugar, and issue another lecture on proper diet and diabetes management, which would once again fall on deaf ears. Hopefully be on her way before either of them ran out of patience.

"Sounds fun," she said with what she hoped was casual

enthusiasm.

Roger offered her a surprisingly wistful smile. "Yeah, it will be. Doug's a great guy. I wish we could hang out more often, but he's in Manhattan, and Bluelick isn't exactly a subway stop away, so…"

His voice held a note of something she worried might be nostalgia. Did he prefer big-city life, with his big-city friends? Were his days in Bluelick numbered? She shook off a wave of alarm. "So, tonight you'll enjoy catching up with an old friend, and I'm pleased to say you'll do it splinter-free." Holding up the tweezers, she showed him the sliver of extracted wood.

"Wow. You've got a gentle touch. I didn't feel a thing."

"Maybe you've got nerves of steel. Should we test the theory with a tetanus shot?"

An adorable little furrow appeared between his brows. "I had one about three weeks ago, when I stepped on a nail on another project. Do I need one again so soon?"

"No. You're fine. You may want to consider another way of contributing to the cause, though. Sounds like building houses is hazardous to your health."

Roger stood and laughed. "You might be right, but I could never bail on Tyler."

"What's Tyler got to do with it?" Even as she asked the question, something toppled from the archives of her memory and drifted to the front of her mind. Last night, when he'd left her place pleading an early-morning commitment, had he mentioned Ashland?

"He's our foreman. He donates time and money to several Habitat projects a year. His construction firm does well, and this is his way of giving back. I figure the least I can do is show up and lend a hand."

"In that case, better add work gloves and some steel-shank boots to your Christmas list."

He grinned. "Right. See you later. Thanks for dealing

with my code red."

She watched him go, mind reeling with the new information. Shame on her, assuming Tyler cut their…uh… *date* short in order to pursue some testosterone-fueled blood sport. Then again, he hadn't said anything about what he was doing, so how could she have known?

She locked up and walked to her car, assimilating what she'd learned about Tyler, and came to the conclusion she needed to adjust her opinion of him. He wasn't an adult version of the hell-raising, trouble-hungry rebel she remembered. He excelled professionally, looked out for his employees and their families—if his loyalty to Junior served as any indication—and did charity work in his spare time. For a man who'd arrived on her doorstep in the wee hours of the morning with a lipstick smear on his shirt and a jealous drunk's bullet in his butt, Tyler Longfoot turned out to be a lot more complex than she expected.

Thirty minutes later she pulled into her father's driveway and noted some things remained exactly as expected. The garbage bin at the curb overflowed with empty beer bottles and fast food cartons. Not the recommended diabetic diet.

Stifling a sigh, she hauled two bags of groceries up the same sagging porch steps she'd spent her younger years imagining led to an enchanted palace, or a lost city or, most fanciful of all, a happy home where two loving parents eagerly awaited her arrival. Adult Ellie harbored no such illusions.

She balanced the bags in one arm and rapped on the screen door, silently cursing the humidity when a bead of sweat trickled into her eye. She muttered a not-so-silent curse when her knock yielded no response. Frank was home. His pickup sat in the cracked asphalt driveway and the TV blared from the other side of the door. She twisted the knob and shoved the door open.

Hot, stale air slapped her as soon as she walked in. She

left the door open, hoping to get a breeze flowing despite the thick air outside. Her father lay sprawled on the faded plaid living room sofa, napping or passed out, with one thin arm flung over his forehead, the other bent across his thickening middle. He looked like he'd slept more than once in his stained wifebeater and rumpled pajama bottoms.

Time hadn't been kind to him. His hair, once the same dark brown she saw in her mirror, was matted and shot with gray. Even in rest, deep lines carved their way across his face. Broken capillaries bloomed around his nose.

How he could sleep with the TV loud enough to be heard in the next galaxy, she didn't know. No, wait, she did know. Six beer bottles littered the cheap wood-grain coffee table.

Because she had a strong impulse to kick the table and send the empties flying, she stomped to the kitchen. She dropped the grocery bags on the chipped and yellowed Formica counter and put the contents away, using the mundane activity to settle her temper. Then she strode back to the living room and turned the TV off. Silence rushed in with deafening intensity.

"Wha' the…?" Frank jerked awake and his bloodshot eyes fixed on her. Good. At least he could still hear. "Hey. I was watching the game."

She tossed the remote toward him. "Really? It kind of looked like you were sleeping. Have you had anything to eat?"

"Yeah," he muttered, picking up the remote.

"Beer doesn't count. I brought groceries. I can make you something."

"I told you, I ate." Not looking at her, he turned the TV on again. Then he lifted his unfinished beer and drank.

"What's your glucose today?" The volume of the game forced her to yell the question. Typical. One way or another, he made communicating impossible.

"Don't remember."

"Where's your meter? It logs every test."

He ignored the question. She reached over and grabbed the beer. He held on. Unwilling to forfeit the ridiculous tug-of-war, she pulled harder.

The bottle popped out of his hand and the sudden, unopposed momentum sent it smacking into her forehead, showering her with beer in the process.

"Damn it, Frank!" She mopped her face with shaking hands. "You can't drink like this on your meds. It's a fast track to liver failure."

"Jesus, stop lecturing me. If you were any kind of a woman, you'd have found a man to hassle by now and leave me alone. Your mother was married with a kid by your age."

And dead by the time she was thirty. But I'm still here. If you'd pull your stubborn head out of your ass and notice I'm here, trying to be your daughter, maybe I wouldn't have to force myself to visit once a week. Rather than voice thoughts he wouldn't know what to do with anyway, she returned to the kitchen and rummaged around in the junk drawer for his glucose meter.

There was no point letting his attitude upset her. Years ago a sharp truth had lodged in the soft underbelly of her heart. Frank had never been interested in fatherhood. Her mom had wanted a child and he'd relented. But after she died, his bitterness over the loss left no room for anyone else, including his own grieving daughter.

Her father's diabetes had been a major factor in her decision to return home to open her practice. She'd harbored a hope that by being here as an adult, helping him, she'd magically break through his barriers and turn them into a real family. But the last couple weeks had driven home a harsh fact. A grown daughter didn't interest Frank either. If she wanted a happy, loving family, her best shot involved turning herself into Roger's dream girl, and then showing him they were made for each other.

Her fingers finally closed over the glucose meter. Reviewing the log didn't take long— one test today, one yesterday, and a handful over the past week. The numbers were high, but not horrible. She opened the kitchen cabinet and checked his supply of meds. He seemed to be taking them as directed.

She spent another five minutes using some of the fresh vegetables she'd bought to make a large salad and placed it in the nearly empty fridge, beside the diabetic-friendly Dijon vinaigrette. Considering her duty done, she washed up and headed to the front room. Her chances of getting so much as a thank-you from her father were nonexistent, but still, she paused at the open door. "I made you a salad. It's in the fridge."

"I hope you brought beer. I'm low."

She pushed open the screen door. "Bye, Frank."

The rickety metal door slammed shut behind her.

Back in her car, she pumped the air-conditioning as high as it would go and looked at herself in the rearview mirror. Her flushed, sweaty reflection stared back, bitter eyes shimmering with unshed tears. A snippet from one of her favorite daydreams flashed through her mind. Roger, running behind a downy-haired Roger III astride a little red bicycle, cheering enthusiastically as the boy pedaled with all his might and slipped free of his father's steadying hands for a first solo ride down the sidewalk.

She closed her eyes and tried to put herself in the picture somewhere, but the image kept fading. She didn't subscribe to fate or destiny, but nonetheless wondered if her inability to visualize herself in her ideal future meant she wasn't destined to be part of such an idyllic family scene. Sure, Roger was the man of *her* dreams, but if she didn't get her lessons back on schedule, he'd be scooped up by some naturally sexy woman before she mastered chapter 3, much less the whole array of skills necessary to turn her into the woman of *his* dreams.

Cool air from the vent blasted her face hard enough to blow her hair off her forehead, revealing a raised red bump near her hairline. Terrific. A memento from the beer bottle.

No good deed went unpunished.

She finger-combed her hair so a frizzy wave covered the ugly spot. Then she backed out of her father's driveway, turned onto the main road, and considered her meager options for Saturday night. Pay bills, catch up on her medical journals, or maybe indulge in her secret guilty pleasure—snuggling in with her DVR and watching the cute host of the home improvement show she recorded religiously? All her choices sounded pathetic. What she really wanted was a drink, but imbibing alone at home in front of the TV seemed a little too much like Frank for comfort.

Just then, the barrel-shaped sign for Rawley's Pub came into view, and before her brain completely vetted the impulse, she pulled into the parking lot.

Chapter Eight

Tyler followed Junior into Rawley's on Saturday night, ready to faithfully execute his role as wingman. Hopefully in the process, he'd get his brain off Ellie. She'd been taking up headspace ever since she'd unleashed her proposition on him. Not surprising. When an intelligent, attractive woman bartered with him for sex education, turns out he gave the arrangement some passing thought. But since yesterday evening, his thoughts weren't just passing. They took a very specific path—namely, how many days, hours, and minutes until their next session. A week seemed way too long to wait.

This disturbed him for a lot of reasons, not the least of which was that in her mind, their relationship had a specific purpose and timeline. Although she hadn't admitted it, he still felt sure she aimed to impress someone particular with her new tricks. Who, he couldn't say, but it wasn't him. She'd selected him as her teacher, not her target. Both the timeline, and the fact that she had her sights set on someone else, rubbed him wrong.

They shouldn't have. A friggin' fantasy had dropped

right into his lap—weeks of wild, five-star sex with a woman who could make his cock harder than reinforced steel simply by flashing her dimples at him. Nothing could be more straightforward. Easy in, easy out. He liked easy. He liked straightforward. Why overcomplicate this scenario with pride or some stupid notion about taking himself, and his relationships, more seriously?

Before he could start chewing on the question again, Junior drew up short and slapped his shoulder.

"There she is. Think she's still pissed at me?"

He followed Junior's sight line to the center table where tall, stacked Lou Ann held court in a low-cut black tank top that showed off the double-Ds like nobody's business. Her eyes narrowed dangerously at the sight of Junior. Melody sat to Lou Ann's left, wearing a peach sundress, looking calm, cool, and bored out of her mind. Flame-haired Ginny occupied the chair on Lou Ann's right, predatory eyes flashing with interest.

He glanced over at Junior, a tugboat of a guy in a Wildcats jersey and baggy jeans. "*I'm* not still pissed at you, and you shot me. Talking Lou Ann out of her mad ought to be simple in comparison."

"Right. You're right." Junior inhaled and let the breath out slowly. "Okay. I'm going in. Cover me."

"I'll be in the corner." Self-preservation had him hanging back at his end of the bar as Ginny slid off her chair and headed toward him. Her tight, copper-colored cropped top and low-slung jeans advertised frighteningly toned abs. The little redhead was as pretty as a shiny new penny, but her reputation as a turbo gossip always turned him off—even more so now that he was trying to show Bluelick Savings and Loan what a responsible, respectable citizen he was. He turned to the bar and tried to make himself invisible, wondering for the billionth time what Ellie was up to tonight.

A throaty voice ambushed him. "Hey Tyler, what's up?"

Resigned, he forced his shoulders to relax and turned back around. "Hey. Not much."

The redhead's grin turned conspiratorial and she tipped her head toward the table behind her. "Check it out. Melody's back in circulation. You heard she and Roger called the engagement off, right?"

He nodded and signaled to Jeb Rawley behind the bar. "Yeah, I heard."

Ginny reminded him of a cat—irresistibly drawn to those who showed the least interest. This maybe accounted for why, somewhere in his reply, she heard a request for details.

"But do you know why?" Before he could tell her he didn't much care, she linked arms with him, snuggled in close and continued, "Roger and Melody were, shall we say, sexually incompatible."

Damn him, but that caught his attention. For a girl born and bred to the prom queen crown, Melody was actually a nice person. Same went for star pitcher, star quarterback, star center Roger. Superficially, they made the perfect blond-haired, blue-eyed, all-American couple, but the way their engagement had dragged out over ten years? The cynical voice in his head had called the wedding off a long time ago. "You don't say."

Jeb paused in front of them long enough to deliver Tyler's regular order—a beer. Ginny waited until Jeb walked away and then dished up more dirt.

"I do," she nodded solemnly, but her eyes practically danced with glee at the prospect of revealing someone else's intimate secrets. "All those years Roger spent away turned him into some kind of wild, insatiable sex maniac. Melody told me he's into a bunch of stuff she flat-out refuses to do. So she wished him luck finding his perfect nymphomaniac soul mate and they went their separate ways—far as any two people can in a town this size."

Okay, that smelled more like bullshit than pay dirt. Ginny's story didn't add up. No way had it taken Melody and Roger a decade to figure out they had incompatible sexual appetites.

What *did* possibly add up was why Ellie suddenly wanted a crash course in Wild Woman 101. Rumors spread like wildfire around Bluelick. Had she heard this one already, taken it as gospel, and decided to learn the skills she thought she needed to satisfy Roger?

The notion left a strange hollow feeling in his stomach and a bad taste in his mouth. Maybe he didn't want to know.

Straightforward, he reminded himself, and took a drink. Uncomplicated. Why make things messy? Speaking of messy...he checked on Junior's progress with Lou Ann. He'd hunkered down in the chair Melody had wisely vacated and appeared to be meekly accepting the verbal whoop-ass Lou Ann was doling out. A good sign, Tyler decided, because Junior had it coming and she wasn't likely to pick things up with him unless she got it out of her system.

His gaze wandered around the packed pub and stopped short. Ellie sat at the other end of the bar, dark waves framing her flawless profile as she smiled up at Jeb and accepted the glass of white wine he placed in front of her. Despite the thirsty crowd, Jeb lingered, wearing the shit-eating grin he insisted made him look like Tom Cruise.

"Something caught your eye, Tyler?"

Ginny's question pulled his attention back to the redhead, who was now watching him with keen interest. He knew better than to give her anything to speculate on. "Just mulling over what you said about Melody and Roger. It sounds a little far-fetched to me. Those two have been joined at the hip since high school. I can't believe it took this long for them to discover he wants triple-X action in the bedroom and she's not willing to go a notch above PG-13. Where'd you get your information?"

"Straight from Melody," she shot back. "You know I don't spread rumors."

"'Course you don't." Unable to stop himself, he let his gaze drift back to Ellie...and Jeb.

"Telling people I saw you and Ellie Swann cruising out to the river on your bike last night, saying y'all looked real snug—that would be spreading a rumor."

It took some effort, but he kept his poker face in place... he hoped. "Good thing you're not like that, huh?"

"I know. I mean, just 'cause something looks like a hookup doesn't mean there isn't some other explanation."

"Exactly," he agreed and took a drink of his beer.

"For all I know, you're her patient. I mean, I've got eyewitnesses saying a week ago Junior stumbled in here at last call, saw Lou Ann cozying up to you, and shot your nuts off."

He nearly choked on his beer. "Jesus, Ginny, where do you hear this crap? Your so-called eyewitnesses are worthless drunks."

She laughed. "Talk is cheap, Tyler. You'll have to do better than a verbal denial if you want to dispute my facts." She turned away, and threw him a challenging smile from over her shoulder. "Any time you want to prove Junior didn't turn you from a stud to a gelding with one well-placed bullet, I'm available for a demonstration."

Not tempting. Elbows propped on the bar, he crossed his ankles and smiled back. "It'd take a much bigger caliber than Junior's overblown BB gun to put a ding in my family jewels."

Ginny merely shrugged and kept walking. Tyler pinched the bridge of his nose to ease the slight headache settling there and wondered how many people sitting in Rawley's tonight seriously thought he couldn't lay pipe anymore. What the hell. He really didn't care, he decided, as he straightened and steered toward the one person in Bluelick who knew his equipment functioned just fine.

Jeb laughed at something Ellie said and slid his hand over her forearm. Tyler decided enough was enough and quickened his pace. He refused to believe Jeb Rawley had inspired her recent interest in sex education. Jeb had never done anything in his lazy life except practice his smirk and wait to inherit his daddy's bar. And if she wanted to perfect the art of the barstool seduction, well, fine, but she already had a practice partner.

He drew up behind Ellie and placed a proprietary hand on her shoulder. One glance at Jeb confirmed the bartender got the message, because he straightened and removed his paw from her arm. Ellie turned those dark maple-and-molasses eyes on him, and for a moment, he simply fell into them.

"Tyler, hi."

"Hey Ty," Jeb echoed, far less enthusiastically. "Another beer?"

Tyler claimed the empty barstool beside Ellie, held up his mostly full bottle, and said, "I'm good," keeping his eyes on her the entire time. Although it was a Saturday, she looked as if she'd come from her office, easily outclassing the jeans and T-shirt crowd at the pub. A sleeveless blouse the exact shade as her eyes left her arms and shoulders bare. A sleek, tan skirt stopped high enough to showcase her gorgeous legs. Ice-pick-thin heels suggested she didn't plan to do a lot of running around.

"What brings you to Rawley's, Doc? Looking to buy someone a drink, make small talk, and…?"

"No, I've seen how that turns out and I didn't wear my Kevlar underwear." Her lips curved, but the amusement didn't reach her eyes, which looked shadowed and a little sad.

Before he could offer a snappy comeback, Melody walked up. "Imagine seeing the two of you here together." The blonde nudged his shoulder playfully. He nudged back, but his playful feeling fizzled when Ellie immediately said, "Oh, we're not together. We just ran into each other. Complete coincidence, right Tyler?"

Melody gave them a smile that made the Mona Lisa look like a grinning fool. "Interesting how that works sometimes, isn't it? Y'all have a good night. I've got to…um…find Ginny."

Ellie frowned as Melody sashayed away. "Sorry, I think she got the wrong idea after walking in on us the other day. I tried to set her straight, but I guess I didn't quite get the message across."

"What message?" He couldn't care less what anybody thought about their relationship, but he wasn't too flattered by Ellie rushing to correct Melody. What was "the wrong idea" anyway, damn it?

"I told her we're not romantically involved, that our relationship is, well…" She lifted one slim shoulder and let it drop.

"Purely academic?" he suggested drily, realizing everything she said, while technically correct, bothered the hell out of him. And the fact that it bothered him bothered him even more.

"No! Of course not. I'd never tell her such a thing. But whatever I said, it fell short of convincing, because she obviously thinks you're interested in me."

He hadn't quite worked out why that was such a horrible, unacceptable thing, when she laughed and nodded down the bar. "For someone in such a hurry to catch Ginny, Melody got easily sidetracked."

Tyler looked over and saw Melody standing with Fire Chief Bradley, giggling prettily at something he said to her. The chief, one of Bluelick's newest residents, had relocated a few months earlier after spending nearly a decade as a deputy chief in Cincinnati.

"She's a free agent now."

Ellie nodded, and the soft glow from the bar lights caught chestnut tones in her hair. "I don't know him except to say hello, but he seems very different from Roger—more the strong, silent type."

Did she like the strong, silent type? "Hmm."

"I mean, I understand his appeal. According to Melody, he's single, available, and gorgeous enough to have graced the pages of the Cincinnati firefighters' fund-raiser calendar every year of his tenure in the department." Holding fingers in front her, she added, "Three times as the cover."

Jeez, listen to her rhapsodize over the guy. Maybe Chief Bradley was the inspiration for Ellie's quest to enhance her sexual skills?

An unfamiliar sensation singed his gut like cheap whiskey. What the hell was wrong with him? One minute he's convinced she's after Roger, the next, Chief Bradley. *Jealousy*, a voice in his head whispered, but he immediately dismissed the notion. He didn't do jealousy. He avoided volatile emotions of any kind. Having grown up with a front row seat to his father's unstable temper, he didn't plan on turning his own life into the same kind of freak show. So why was he suddenly ready to strangle the fire chief with his bare hands just because Ellie found the guy "appealing"? The humidity was making him edgy, that was all.

"Oh my, I guess Lou Ann and Junior made up."

Happy for a distraction, Tyler followed her gaze to the alcove by the pool table and decided she had a gift for understatement. Lou Ann and Junior looked about halfway to make-up sex in their not-so-dark corner. Junior's hands were all over the seat of Lou Ann's painted-on jeans, and she'd plastered herself against his chest so tightly the double-

Ds threatened to spill out of her tank top.

Ellie patted his hand. "Sorry."

"What for, Doc?"

"I know you were, ah, *interested* in her. I guess you missed your window of opportunity."

Tyler stared at his beer and shrugged. "I'm not *interested* in Lou Ann. The only reason we gave each other a second glance was because Junior managed to piss her off and I was too bored to question her motives when she started talking to me. I'm glad they've patched things up."

"Well, for your butt's sake, I hope you don't get bored again anytime soon."

"Honey, I haven't been bored since you turned up."

The comment earned him a smile, but it didn't quite chase the wounded look from her eyes.

"How about you, Doc? It that why you're here tonight? Boredom?"

"No, I wanted to get away from"—she sighed and moved her hands restlessly on the bar—"*stuff* for a while."

He took a sip of his beer and inspected her face. Yeah, something troubled her. The corners of her extremely kissable mouth kept wilting.

He had a reputation for keeping things light, superficial even, and minding his own business, so he couldn't really explain what made him tug her stool closer and prod. "Tough day at the office?"

"No. Easy day. One splinterectomy, but it was a complete success."

"So why aren't you celebrating your surgical triumph?"

She lifted a shoulder and let it drop in a gesture that managed to convey both frustration and resignation. "I stopped by to see Frank afterward. The visit kind of sucked the triumph right out of me." She aimed a tight smile at him. "Enough said on that topic."

Well, hell. Frank was a bitter, self-absorbed bastard and a sorry excuse for a father. And Tyler considered himself an expert on lousy dads. Living with Big Joe had equated to sharing space with a rabid Rottweiler. He'd made himself scarce until the second he turned eighteen, and then officially got the fuck out. When Joe had tipped over from a heart attack a few years later, Tyler had figured he was finally done with the man, but unfortunately, losing his father was like losing a limb. Sometimes he still woke up in a cold sweat, reeling from the phantom pain of beefy fists pummeling him.

Frank, however, still lived and breathed, and as certain men would do, aimed his foul mood at his offspring. Tyler sympathized with her situation, even as he told himself to stay out of it. She clearly wasn't looking for sympathy and didn't seem keen on sharing details. He respected her desire to keep her own counsel. Having just gotten an earful of Melody and Roger's sex issues as well as the latest gossip concerning his own maligned manhood, he understood the advantages of discretion. Why her silence left him vaguely disappointed and wondering if she ever confided in anyone, he couldn't say. God knows they had far better things to discuss than Frank.

The humidity had kicked Ellie's waves up a notch—closer to the wild tangle he remembered. Absently, he tucked a stray tendril behind her ear and spotted the small mark on her forehead.

"What's this?"

"What's what?" She glanced at him uncertainly, but her cheeks went up in flames when he ran his finger over the tender spot near her hairline. "It's nothing. You can thank Frank for that."

A fist gripped his gut and his vision actually hazed for an instant. He carefully placed his half-empty beer on the bar and stood. "I believe I will," he said softly.

"What?" Her brow creased as she worked out the

meaning of his reply, then her eyes went wide, and she placed her hand on his forearm. "Tyler, wait."

He shook his head, eased out of her hold and started for the door.

"Wait," she repeated, more urgently this time. Her heels clicked on the wood floor as she hurried after him. When she grabbed his arm again, he took a deep breath to calm the tide of fury rising inside him before it crested and broke all over the wrong person.

She faced him and spoke quickly. "Frank didn't lay a hand on me. I got this cleaning up his pigsty of a living room. One of his empties tried to make a break for it."

He searched her face for a long moment, looking for signs of evasion, but she returned his stare unblinkingly. She was telling the truth—or mostly the truth. Some of the tension seeped out of him. Shifting his attention to her forehead, he skimmed his thumb over the small welt.

"You're not his maid."

She laughed, but the sound held no hint of humor. "Worse. I'm his daughter. I can't even quit."

"Sure you can. You ask me, he quit a long time ago."

"Maybe you're right, and God only knows what kind of loser that makes me, but joyless as it was, he did his duty by me. I always had a roof over my head, food to eat, and a bed to sleep in. I guess I feel compelled to do the same for him now."

Tyler moved his lips over her temple and across her cheekbone. "He's the loser, not you. And you don't owe him a damn thing. His duty went far beyond three squares and a cot."

"You don't understand…" Fingers curled into his belt loops and a hot face pressed into his neck. He felt a sudden, nearly uncontrollable desire to bundle her up in his arms and carry her away—far away.

"Try me."

"God, no." She took a shaky breath, and then pulled back and offered him a stiff smile—no dimples. "It's over and done with. I can't think of a bigger waste of breath." She looked around the bar as if to see if they'd attracted any unwanted attention—they hadn't—and then fixed a determinedly brighter smile on her face. "Like I said, I'm here to get away."

Screw precautions. Her reasons for wanting to expand her sexual repertoire didn't matter to him as much as finding a way to erase the shadows from her face. Moving closer, he toyed with the trio of small gold leaves dangling from her earlobe. "I know a foolproof getaway plan, if you're interested."

Her eyes zoomed to his. "Could we complete lesson one?"

Shit, he should have known the prospect of getting back on schedule would tempt her. "If you want." For starters.

"My place?"

"No, my place. The best getaways involve a new destination," he argued when she hesitated. But the truth was, he wanted her in his bed, for reasons he preferred not to think on too deeply. "C'mon." He took her hand and led her out of the pub.

"My car..."

"I'll drive you back in the morning."

She cringed. "No. I'll follow you. People don't want to see the town doctor's car parked all night at a bar. Bluelick's grapevine thrives on tidbits like whose car was parked at Rawley's after closing on a Saturday night."

Shit. She had a point. And as he acknowledged it, very entertaining notions about spending the drive discovering exactly what she had on under her tight little skirt dissolved. "Okay, follow me to my place."

Chapter Nine

Ellie kept her eyes on Tyler's black pickup while her mind frantically reviewed the finer points of chapter 3. Finally, an opportunity to put her studies into practice, and she wanted to get everything exactly right. Excitement and nerves tangoed in her stomach, and not just because this represented a first step toward achieving her long-term goal of winning Roger's heart. It also had to do with Tyler. She was attracted to him—physically, of course—but in other ways, too. He made her laugh. He challenged her. Coming up short in his eyes would be mortifying. Bottom line? She cared what he thought.

The realization surprised her, but then again, he was full of surprises. Nobody, ever, in her entire life, had displayed a single protective instinct toward her. Back at Rawley's when he'd stalked toward the door like a dark knight about to slay her dragon, he'd shocked the hell out of her—and stirred something deep inside her heart. Whatever it was, she harbored a small fear she'd never quite push it back into place.

You will, her logical mind insisted. She'd always taken

care of herself, pursued her goals on her own, and slain her own dragons. How? By making plans and sticking to them. Which brought her right back to chapter 3. Once again she called up the details she'd committed to memory and quizzed herself.

But when she followed Tyler's truck down a narrow, oak-canopied driveway and pulled up in front of his house, the lesson plan in her head faded. She didn't register stopping her car or stepping out. The graceful slopes and angles of the beautifully restored wood-and-brick Victorian in front of her commanded her full attention, from the custom-turned rails in the big, wraparound porch to each painstakingly fitted shingle on the dominant front gable.

She sensed rather than saw Tyler approach, because she couldn't tear her eyes away from the house. "Incredible. Like a storybook—"

He brought his mouth down on hers. While he kissed her until her head spun, he maneuvered her up the front steps. Lips still busy on hers, he worked the old lock on the front door and then shoved her into the hall.

She broke away for air, but couldn't resist angling her head to see more of the interior. All she could make out in the dim light were creamy plaster walls and lots of dark wood trim. "Your house is amazing."

He nuzzled her ear. "I almost forget the blood, sweat, and tears this place cost me when you look at it like that."

"I love big, old homes. I think owning one must be like becoming part of a family. Can I look around?" Her voice caught on the question when he backed her up against the door. Her handbag hit the polished oak floor with a soft thud.

"I'll give you the tour later, if you're a good girl." His hands skimmed up her abdomen until his fingertips encountered the underwire of her bra. He shifted the cups just enough to make her shiver, despite the heat.

"A good girl?" she managed as his hands ran over her, lighting fires everywhere they touched. "Longfoot, you're letting the whole teacher/student thing go to your head."

"It's gone somewhere, but I don't think you're going to complain." His hands sneaked under her skirt and into the back of her panties. He hauled her up against him, and she quickly realized the only complaint she had was that she couldn't get close enough. Animal instinct kicked in and she climbed up his big, solid frame. Arms locked around his neck, legs wrapped around his waist, she rocked against him, not caring that her skirt was bunched up at her hips.

Seconds later, he had her blouse unbuttoned and her bra shoved aside. She held her breath as he cupped her breast and growled appreciatively. She knew she didn't have a whole lot to appreciate, and generally preferred if guys left her breasts out of the proceedings, but Tyler didn't squeeze and knead them like bread dough. No, he smoothed and caressed and lavished attention on her understated curves until her nipples tightened to sensitive peaks. The scrape of his rough palms made her thighs clench. When he caught the hard beads between his long fingers and pinched lightly, she felt the tug all the way to her core.

Oh God, if she didn't do something fast, he was going to take her completely off her plan again. With strength born of desperation, she wriggled out of his hold and slapped her palm against the center of his chest. "Not so fast, Tyler. We're covering chapter 3, remember?"

"Fine by me." Keeping his eyes locked on hers, he dropped to his knees in front of her.

"What are you—?"

"Better hold on." He curved his hand under her hip, supporting her, and shrugged her thigh over his shoulder. The move forced her off-balance. She scrambled for a handhold along the rock-hard muscle of his other shoulder.

"This isn't chapter 3," she protested as he brushed his lips over her thigh.

"Sure it is." Lightly, he bit the other, and then followed up with a kiss.

Then he kissed in between. Her neck muscles dissolved and her head hit the door with a clunk.

His tongue traced the edge of her panties and delved beneath. She switched her grip from his shoulder to the top of his head, not sure if she meant to stop him or give him encouragement. He took it as encouragement, and sent his incredibly talented tongue on another pass.

"Tyler…" Was that whimper really her? "Y-you've got things backward."

Through half-closed eyes she saw him smile. His grip on her backside tightened. "Backward, my ass. Sparky, prepare yourself for a lesson you'll never forget."

. . .

Tyler heard his bossy student whisper, "Wait," when he moved in for the kill, but he ignored her. No more waiting. He went in—fast and furious and more than a little out of control. Her fingers plunged into his hair and twisted so hard he figured he'd have a bald patch by the time she finished, and he really didn't give a shit. The way she rocked her hips and pushed herself against his tongue tipped him off that she didn't either. Hell, she was off to the races. He leaned in, using his weight to trap her hips tighter between him and the door, and did his damnedest to keep the pace so urgent she wouldn't have time to think.

He quickly discovered that, for Sparky, not being able to think didn't mean not being able to talk, because her breathless monologue reached his ears.

"Oh…God. That feels amazing, but I can't—

"You can. Thirty seconds, tops." To prove his point, he flicked his tongue dangerously close to the bull's-eye.

She jerked and let out a tortured little moan, but still had the gall to argue with him. "I never can, not even during a reverse chapter 3. Don't take it personal…"

Determined to render her speechless, not to mention just plain wrong, he adjusted his grip on her hips, closed his mouth around her slick, swollen clit, and sucked until her entire body trembled.

"Ohmigod! Oh…my…God. I think I'm going to—

Hell, yeah, you are. But before he could send her over, Beethoven's Fifth chimed from somewhere by her feet. *What the…?* A reluctant glance down confirmed what he already suspected. The symphony came from her handbag. He looked up at her, silently questioning.

She was a sight to behold. Eyes closed, lips parted, looking sweaty, flushed, and incredibly beautiful.

The symphony chimed again. She let out a long, slow, shaky breath, muttering something about being cursed to a life of solo orgasms. Then those big, dazed eyes opened and landed on him, brimming with disappointment. "That's probably my service."

"I was afraid you were going to say something like that." Doing his best to pretend the sinking sensation in his chest stemmed from his heart pumping blood, double-time, to his highly frustrated dick, he scooped her bag off the floor and handed it to her, then slowly eased to his feet.

"No, no. Don't get up! You never know—this could be a quick question about a prescription."

"I'm not going anywhere, Doc."

She sent him a grateful look and dug around in that big bag of hers for her phone while simultaneously attempting to push her skirt down. He couldn't offer much help with a medical matter, but getting a woman in and out of her skirt?

Different story. He took over the chore—and took his time with it—while she concentrated on her call. By the time she finished, he was really just entertaining himself, using the job of smoothing her skirt as an excuse to run his palms over the perfect handful of her ass.

"I'm sorry, Tyler." She tossed her phone into her bag, avoiding his eyes, and got to work refastening her bra. "I have to go. A patient's baby girl spiked a 103-degree fever. I'm meeting them at my office."

"No need to be sorry." Though he was, incredibly, as he watched her tuck her pretty little breasts away behind her pretty little bra. "Every once in a while it's bound to happen—someone's gonna need you even more than I do."

He'd meant the comment as a glib reference to the minor medical emergency still straining the front of his jeans, but the whole "need you" part came out strangely serious. It gave him pause. Her, too, apparently, because her fingers fumbled on her blouse buttons.

"Thanks," she said, giving the task of buttoning her blouse far more concentration than it warranted. "That's sweet of you—a charming reaction to a distinctly un-charming situation. Unfortunately, we're getting nowhere fast on my educational goals. If I don't start mastering some skills soon, it's going to be too late."

Sweet? Had she really just called him *sweet*? He drove a Harley, for Christ's sake. He got shot at in bars. Not on a regular basis, no, but if nothing else, taking a bullet in the ass ought to mean nobody called him sweet. Next she'd be calling him *nice*, and if that happened, he might as well tie a big pink bow around his balls and hand them over. On top of all that, what the fuck was up with the "too late" business?

He flattened his palms on the door, trapping her, and leaned in close. "Too late for what? Tell me, Ellie, before you scoot out my door. Is the world going to explode?"

Unwanted images of her wrapped around Roger, and then Chief Bradley, burned in his mind, and set a nasty little fire in the pit of his stomach. "Or is somebody going to switch status from 'available' to 'off the market' before you can make a move?"

Wide, worried eyes flew to his, and then quickly shifted away. *Bingo*, he thought, for once hating to be right.

"I ..." she swallowed and started again. "I have a schedule I want to stick to. Like any self-improvement effort, it's important to keep the momentum. I'm not blaming you, Tyler." Her eyes darted back to him and she smiled weakly. "I mean, tonight's interruption isn't your fault. I just thought we'd have at least one lesson completed by now."

"Momentum. I see." He reached behind her and opened the door. She wanted momentum? He'd give her so much freaking momentum that she'd get completely caught up in the ride and forget where she planned on going. "In that case, what are you doing Tuesday night?"

She blinked. "Nothing."

"Feel like taking a shopping trip to Lexington?"

"Chapter 6?"

"Yep."

Her loud gulp almost made him laugh out loud. Now who was sweet?

"Okay," she said, but he noticed the bravado in her voice didn't match her round eyes and pink cheeks. Momentum restored, just like that.

Yet as he watched her taillights disappear down his drive, he couldn't help wondering if he'd just let his student get the better of him.

• • •

Tuesday afternoon, Ellie raised her head from her chart

notes when her office door opened. Melody stepped inside. Normally smooth, blond waves tumbled chaotically around a face past due for a powder and lipstick touch-up. Her once crisp white blouse and swingy yellow skirt bore creases and a few unidentifiable stains. Still, Ellie had to admit, Melody looked sexily disheveled. Meanwhile *she* probably looked like she'd spent the afternoon in a sweatbox.

Melody closed the door, adjusted one of the framed diplomas on the wall, and then plopped down in one of the pair of forest-green upholstered guest chairs opposite the desk. "Whew! What a day. I swear it felt like Grand Central Station in here an hour ago."

Ellie propped her elbows on her big, orderly polished walnut desk. "Nothing fills exam rooms like an outbreak of hand, foot, and mouth virus among the preschool set. You did an amazing job handling the onslaught."

The blonde shrugged off the praise, but smiled. "The little ones are super-cute, and I'm glad it turned out to be nothing serious. But we had a packed schedule *before* the panicked mommy calls started. Squeezing an extra six patients in at the last minute, making up the charts, collecting the insurance information and co-pays—I won't mind if we don't see a rush like that again for a while."

"Me either. Are they all gone?"

"Yep. We're officially done for the day. I don't know about you, but my bathtub and I are going to spend some quality time together."

"You wild woman," Ellie teased.

"Hey, you never know." Melody got to her feet and winked. "I might see if my bunny swims."

"You have a pet rabbit?"

"No. Come on, Ellie, you know...*The Bunny*."

When Ellie shook her head, Melody's eyes rounded. "Oh, my God! You've somehow missed out on the single girl's best friend. Do yourself a favor and Google it. Have your credit card handy. You won't be sorry."

"Um. Okay. Thanks. Have a good night."

"You too, honey. Though unless you pony up for next-day delivery, you'll have to wait five to seven business days before you have a good night."

Curiosity got the better of her. As soon as she heard the outer door close, she turned to her computer, launched Explorer and typed "the bunny" into her search engine. Within minutes she found herself in a new and heretofore unexplored world of vibrating elastomer personal toys. Fascinated, she clicked on various styles, reading the product descriptions, the specs, and customer reviews. She had to admit all the sizes, colors, and…mercy…the capabilities of the darn thing intrigued her, and frankly, turned her on, but the idea of stimulating herself to orgasm without the benefit of Tyler's lips, hands, and a few other essential parts seemed hollow—like getting an A on a book report by skimming the CliffsNotes instead of reading the book.

If the user reviews could be believed, scores of satisfied customers disagreed. One particularly enthusiastic review had her slouched in her chair, fanning her cheeks.

"Must be a helluva website to put that look on your face, Doc."

Ellie nearly fell out of her chair. She jerked upright and saw Tyler standing in her doorway, looking tall and tanned and entirely too cool. She grabbed a pen and pulled a chart from the stack on her desk. "Jesus. You scared me."

"Sorry. I wasn't trying to sneak up on you. Guess you were too engrossed in…" Before she could stop him, he rounded her desk and peered at her computer screen. "Ah, well. This explains things. Making up a personal shopping list for our field trip this evening?"

"No. I was merely doing some research." Though she

strived for dignity, heat flooded her face. Stupid to be embarrassed. Tyler already knew about her plan to master at least five sexual tactics designed to bring a man to his knees. But for whatever reason, it unnerved her to be caught indulging her curiosity about something not on their curriculum, and not centered on pleasing a partner.

"Uh-huh." He relaxed against her desk, facing her, and stared pointedly at her chest, where her nipples were on high alert. "Looks to me like you were enjoying your research."

She crossed her arms over her chest and lied. "It's a little cool in here, that's all." The room felt hot—surface-of-the-sun hot.

Tyler laughed and pulled her to her feet. "Maybe we should crank up the heat a little?" Then he lowered his head and brushed his lips slowly, purposefully over hers. Her eyelids drifted down, and things definitely warmed up. Her breasts melted against the solid wall of his chest. Her stomach fluttered against his carved-from-granite abs. He slid his hand down her spine, pressing their lower bodies together until a moan vibrated in the back of her throat.

Tyler groaned and said something she didn't catch, and then pulled away. She curled her hand around his neck and went onto her tiptoes in hot pursuit, but came up empty.

"Huh?" She forced her eyes open and stared at him.

He rested his hands on her shoulders, brought his forehead to hers, and gave her a slow, lazy smile. "We get any hotter, and I'm thinking our shopping trip won't happen."

She blinked. The shopping trip. How could she have forgotten? "Of course." She straightened and ran an unsteady hand over her skinny black skirt. "We should get going."

Tyler stepped aside and let her precede him. "That's what I figured."

"I'll drive," she said, struggling for some small measure of control. As usual, Tyler had fogged her brain the minute he'd aimed his devastating smile at her.

It had to stop. This wasn't supposed to be about what *she* liked, or what drove *her* headlong into mindless pleasure—something he managed to explore with breathtaking results every single time she tried to complete her carefully planned lessons. The sensual vortex he sucked her into stirred up her hormones, but also, and more worrisome, her emotions. Maybe he wasn't doing it intentionally, but all the seduction he directed her way threatened her focus. Her goal wasn't to lose herself in Tyler Longfoot.

Absolutely not. What would be stupider than falling for Bluelick's resident playboy? She needed his help perfecting the techniques she'd use to woo Roger. All she had to do was stick to her plan.

Frustrated with herself, Ellie turned and glanced at Tyler, who was now giving her an odd look.

She forced a casual laugh. "I'm sorry. Did you say something?"

He smiled back. "I said, 'Whatever you want,' Doc."

Chapter Ten

Tyler had a hard time keeping up his end of the conversation, what with his life flashing before his eyes. Ellie steered them down Highway 68 toward Lexington, nearly giving him whiplash as she streaked in and out of traffic. Good thing she lived and worked in the same town, because Ellie on the open highway was an accident waiting to happen.

"Look," she sighed. "There's the Browning farm. I've always loved that place."

"I'm trying to buy it." The words spilled out of his mouth like a deathbed confession as she weaved between two SUVs.

"For real? Like, fix it up and live there?"

He closed his eyes and nodded. "Fix it up and sell it."

"I can't wait to see the finished product. When do you start?"

"Soon as I get the construction loan. Unfortunately, Bluelick Savings has some reservations."

"Why? Haven't they seen your work? You're the only person on earth who would do the place justice."

Her faith in his skill humbled him, even more than her

driving terrified him. He pried his eyes open and looked over at her. "Let's just say they're concerned about my risk profile," which increased exponentially with every minute spent in her passenger seat. "Lenders don't get too excited about forking over a couple million bucks to a guy who gets shot in a bar."

"That's unfair. You were the victim."

"Nonetheless, it distracts from my expertise rehabbing historic structures. I need to show them I'm a stable, responsible investment."

"I can't believe this. You grew up here. You operate a successful business here. If that's not stable, what is? The things you've accomplished took hard work and responsibility. If they can't see that, there's something wrong with them. Could you go to another bank?"

Her outrage smoothed out the worst of his ragged frustration. "I stand the best chance of getting the loan locally." *If I live that long*, he silently added as she accelerated.

She said something in response, but her calm, utterly unconcerned voice faded under the pounding in his ears when she came up fast behind an eighteen-wheeler. He gripped the oh-shit handle and jammed his foot down hard on his imaginary brake as she swerved over the broken yellow center line, where another huge truck barreled down on them from the opposite direction. With seconds to spare before they became roadkill, she passed the rig and dropped her Mini back into their lane. He bit his lip to keep from screaming like a little girl.

His terrified lungs took a minute to unfreeze enough to let him suck in air. Once he resumed breathing, he heard Ellie ask, "Don't you think?"

"Huh?" He made himself loosen his death grip on the handle above the passenger-side window. "Yes, I think I should drive home."

She glanced at him and frowned. "That's not what I

asked. Tyler, are you feeling okay? You look a little pale."

"A near-death experience always leaves me pale." At her confused expression, he tapped the dashboard and said, "I can't believe you were afraid to ride on my bike. You drive this car around as if a collision with anything bigger than a gnat swarm wouldn't turn it into a rolling coffin."

She laughed. "I'll have you know I'm a very good driver. I've never had an accident."

"How many have you *caused*?"

She laughed again and swatted his arm. "None."

"Both hands on the wheel, Leadfoot. This is our exit."

She took the off-ramp. "You're just a bad passenger. You're one of those people who always has to be in the driver's seat."

He shook his head in automatic denial. "That's not true. I'm a very laid-back guy. Ask anyone."

"Yeah, you like people to think you are, but you're not. You're a closet control freak. Tell me, when was the last time you occupied the passenger seat, before today?"

"I ride shotgun all the time."

"Name one."

"Hell, I don't know..." Damned if he could think of an instance off the top of his head. "It's not the kind of thing I keep track of."

"Difficult to keep track of something that never happens."

"Bull— Holy shit, red light!"

"I see it," she said tersely and applied the brake, easily rolling to a stop. Then she shot him an "I rest my case" look. "You're uptight because you're not the one in charge."

He dropped his head back against the seat rest and closed his eyes, silently accepting his fate. "Okay, fine. You're a fabulous driver. The problem is entirely mine."

"The problem goes beyond driving. You're out of practice letting someone else have control, period. I can't believe you don't know this about yourself."

The defensive feeling tried to rush back, but he throttled it because he wanted to hear what she had to say. "For example?"

She hesitated, glanced at him, and then took a deep breath and stared back at the traffic. "Well, during our lessons—or should I say, lesson attempts—you're always the one in charge."

"I'm the teacher."

"Okay, yes, but I'm the one who came up with the lessons, and so far you've refused to follow the plans. Don't give me that innocent look, Tyler. You know exactly what I'm talking about."

He couldn't argue with her there, but her plans were too single-minded and one-way for his taste. "You seemed to be having a good time."

"Well...that's the problem, too," she admitted, turning her gorgeous mouth down in a worried little frown at the same time she turned into the discreetly marked parking lot for Slap & Tickle. "I lose my concentration when you don't stick to the plan. I forget what I'm doing and focus on how *you're* making *me* feel." She parked and threw up her hands.

"And that's a problem?" He asked the question gently, but his heart hammered in his chest. This wasn't some detached, academic pursuit for her. She wanted it to be, but it wasn't. *Thank God*, a voice drawled from somewhere in the back of his head.

"A big problem. I pay no attention to the lesson, my technique, none of it." Shaking her head, she went on. "I'm afraid I'm not going to succeed at"—her eyes drifted away—"what I set out to accomplish."

Fine by him if she didn't succeed. Humiliating as it was to admit, the "other man" part of things was starting to seriously piss him off.

Frustrated with himself, and her, he pushed the thought away. "Unwad your panties, Sparky. You're acing everything so far."

She flinched a little at his sarcasm, and he instantly felt like a dick.

"Right," she said softly, obviously not believing him.

"How can you doubt it? There's a pretty reliable gauge of success right between my legs."

"What happens between your legs can be an almost completely biological reaction, which tells me next to nothing about the quality of the experience or my, um...efforts."

"You want a written evaluation?"

Somehow she managed to look exasperated and more than a little intrigued at the same time, and he couldn't hold on to his annoyance.

"Feedback is always welcome, but mostly I need to get back on plan. For our next session, could you let *me* take the lead, and you just sort of consult as you see the need?"

"I'll give it a shot, Doc."

"Thank you," she said primly, as if they weren't discussing sex rules.

"So, do I need to grade the extracurricular stuff, like those sexy little sounds you make when you're about to come, or are we ready to shop?"

She blushed and opened her door. "I'm ready to shop."

"Oh, and Ellie?"

"Yes?"

"You can take the lead in bed, but I'm driving home."

• • •

Standing in the "Tie Me Up, Tie Me Down" aisle at Slap & Tickle, staring at the mind-boggling selection of restraints on display, Ellie realized Tyler had done it yet again—taken her plans and turned them upside down. So much for the quick, list-driven shopping trip she'd envisioned.

How had he accomplished the feat this time? By bringing her here, where a seemingly simple item like wrist restraints led to a thousand decisions. The variables were astounding, in terms of construction, color, features, and embellishments. Leather or satin or standard-issue handcuffs? Lock and key or buckle or Velcro wrap? Her overstimulated imagination made the choice harder, because she kept picturing Tyler lying across her bed with his wrists bound above his head, completely at her mercy. She'd definitely be in the driver's seat, so to speak. Just thinking about it made her shiver with anticipation.

The only thing she couldn't clearly picture was the type of cuffs. The Velcro ones reminded her of medical restraints, which called to mind every off-the-meds schizophrenic who'd come through the ER during her rotation. Instant buzzkill. The leather belt-style versions looked like too much work.

"Which ones do you want?" he asked.

"I don't know. The book didn't specify and I had no idea there'd be so much variety. Which ones do you like?"

"I guess I'm a traditionalist, 'cause..." He slipped a pair of standard, law-enforcement-style handcuffs off the display rack. "They're the most versatile, if you ever have to make a citizen's arrest."

She nodded, swallowing hard at the updated mental image of Tyler naked, handcuffed to her bed. To hell with the finish on her bed frame. A few more scratches would add character, she decided as he tossed the cuffs into the bordello-red browsing tote he'd snagged from the store's supply on their way in.

They moved on to the "Love is Blind" aisle and she found the selection of blindfolds equally overwhelming. There were full-head hoods, hoods that covered the top half only, traditional blindfolds, and eye masks in every color, texture, and material imaginable. She looked over at Tyler and found him eyeing her.

"Any preference, Doc?"

"Um, something small"—which eliminated the hoods—"simple to put on"—which nixed any options with complicated fasteners, laces, zippers—"and breathable?" Good-bye leather, rubber, latex, and, jeez...pleather. Everything about his face appealed to her and she didn't want whatever they chose to conceal too much of it, especially not his very talented mouth.

"Again with the classics, then." He selected a black silk scarf from the display and added it to their bag. "Let's look over here." Taking her hand, he led her to a perimeter aisle mysteriously named "Ever Ready," but when she saw the display he stopped in front of, she laughed and backed away.

"Oh, no, really. That's not on the shopping list."

Undaunted, he picked up a black box. Hot-pink letters announcing "The Bunny" slashed across the top, and a transparent window revealed an equally pink phallus with a pearl-filled shaft and a bunny-shaped "clit teaser" extending from the base.

"You're the one who wants to expand her horizons. Don't you think you should own"—he read from the box's back panel—"'the indispensable sex accessory for today's sophisticated woman'?"

She shook her head and took another step away, vaguely aware she was entering the archway to one of the special interest rooms. "No impulse buying. I made our shopping list based on the items recommended by my manual, and a vibrator's not anywhere on... Whoops!" She accidentally backed into someone. She turned to apologize to the victim of her hasty retreat, but the words died on her lips. "Oh, my God... Roger!"

"Um... Hi, Ellie." Stunned blue eyes shifted to Tyler, who'd moved to stand beside her. "Hey, Tyler."

She'd never seen someone's color rise so quickly. Roger looked as if he might throw up, or pass out, or both. While he stood there, clearly at a loss for words, a cute, athletic-looking guy stepped around him and extended a hand. "Hi, I'm Doug."

She leaned forward and shook the offered hand. "Roger's friend from law school?"

His smile deepened. Humor danced in his beautiful gray eyes. "I like to tell people I spent those three years in a Turkish prison, but yes, I went to Georgetown with Miss Manners here." He shoulder-checked Roger as he said it, provoking another slightly seasick look. "It's nice to finally meet some of Roger's friends from home."

"Good old Bluelick," Tyler said, returning Doug's handshake. "You never know where we'll turn up."

"In all the best places, obviously," Doug replied, clearly unperturbed to be caught shopping in an adult toy emporium.

Roger didn't share his friend's nonchalance. "We were just...ah..."

"Shopping for a friend's bachelor party," Doug interjected, aiming an impatient look at Roger.

Ellie latched onto the excuse with both hands. "Us, too! Well, a bachelorette party, actually." Then she silently prayed Roger wouldn't ask whose, or she'd have to speed back to Bluelick, point a shotgun at Junior, and force him to propose to Lou Ann.

He didn't ask. He gripped Doug's arm and tugged his friend down the aisle. "We should get going. Let you two get on with your shopping."

"Bye!" Doug called.

"Nice to meet you," she replied as they disappeared around the end of the aisle.

"A bachelorette party?"

"Would you have preferred I let them think we were shopping for ourselves?" she whispered. "They had a perfectly innocent excuse for being here, so I…borrowed it."

"You lied, Doc," Tyler drawled with the superior air of someone standing on the moral high ground—which he somehow managed despite standing in the aisles of a sex shop.

"I lied to save everyone from embarrassment."

"I wasn't embarrassed. In fact, I found the whole situation pretty interesting."

She rolled her eyes and spied a restroom sign in an alcove at the far end of the aisle. "I have to use the ladies' room."

"Take your time." Smiling smugly, he sauntered away.

Alone in the restroom, she dissected every nuance of the encounter with Roger. At first, the pleasure of seeing him had blinded her to the embarrassing predicament of being caught shopping at the Slap & Tickle with Tyler. Sooner or later Roger would figure out there was no bachelorette party and then he'd probably decide she was some kind of kinky nympho. Which, come to think of it, was exactly what she wanted him to believe. Maybe the whole awkward incident was actually a blessing in disguise?

The thought cheered her until she factored Tyler into the equation. Would Roger assume they were seriously involved? No. Everyone in Bluelick knew Tyler Longfoot and "seriously involved" went together like schnapps and pickles. Roger would assume she was the latest in the long line of women Tyler passed the time with. The likelihood he'd think there was anything serious between them hovered somewhere between *hell* and *no*.

All of which should have been a major relief. So why did the thought of being a woman Tyler passed the time with leave her feeling hollow and depressed? She shook her head at her reflection. Tyler specialized in careless fun and didn't pretend otherwise. Hoping for more from him would be like hoping for a display of fatherly interest from Frank—stupid and futile.

Focus on your goal, Ellie. Seeing Roger tonight conceivably brought her one step closer to convincing him they were meant for each other.

By the time she returned to the store Tyler was waiting by the main door, all checked out and ready to go. She hurried over and reached for the shopping bag. "I was going to buy the stuff."

He lifted the bag out of her grasp. "Don't worry about it. I picked up a few things from my own list while you were gone." He held the door open and waited while she walked through.

"What'd you buy?"

"Not gonna tell you."

Now curiosity tickled her brain like an itch she simply *had* to scratch. "Why not?" flew out of her mouth before she could stop herself.

He held out his hand for her car keys. "I'm trying to save everyone from embarrassment."

She handed him the keys. "Yeah, right. You're not the least bit embarrassed." Hiking to the passenger side, she accepted defeat. "Fine, don't tell me what you bought, but at least let me pay you for my things."

"Our things," he corrected, tossing the bag into the back and then hitting the lever to adjust the driver's seat, "and let it be. It's my treat. Hungry?"

"Sure, but dinner's on me," she said as he pulled out of the parking lot.

"Ellie, let's get something straight. I'm not your gigolo. You're not paying me or reimbursing my fucking expenses. Understood?"

"That's not what I think, nor what I'm trying to do." The hint of his temper and her own indignity made her voice shaky. She inhaled a deep, stabilizing breath, exhaled slowly, and continued. "I didn't mean to insult you. I was actually just trying to be fair. I know you wouldn't be spending your time or money this way if not for our deal, and I don't want to take advantage of you."

"That's not true," he replied, but he said it softly, with no heat behind the words.

"What's not true?"

"That I wouldn't spend time with you if not for our deal."

"We've known each other all our lives, and you were never remotely interested in spending time with me before."

"You're four years younger than me. You were jailbait, Doc, and then you were gone."

She poked him in the shoulder. "Now who's lying to save himself embarrassment? You weren't the least bit attracted to me even once in all those years and you damn well know it."

He had the grace to look chastised. "You *were* kind of a late bloomer."

She sat back in her seat, crossed her arms over her chest, and found herself stifling a grin. She'd looked like a nearsighted scarecrow in a fright wig most of her adolescence. The idea of the nerdy girl she'd been attracting him…well, she couldn't hold back the unwilling laugh. "I had better things to do than chase boys anyway."

"Doc?"

"What?"

"Late or not, you bloomed just fine. I enjoy spending time with you, and it's got nothing to do with our deal."

Surprised, she stared out the window and smiled. It was, quite possibly, the nicest thing anyone had ever said to her.

Chapter Eleven

Ellie stayed uncharacteristically quiet during dinner. The restaurant's wall frescoes of gondoliers steering their boats along Venetian canals appeared to have captured her attention, but Tyler suspected she was thinking about their encounter with Roger.

He'd stood in the aisle at Slap & Tickle, watching a myriad of emotions play across her face. First had been surprise, followed quickly by a glow of pleasure, and then the awkward awareness of exactly where they all were and the dicey implications. She'd been so desperate to offer up an excuse for being there, with him, she'd told a fib—a rickety one at best, because no parties happened in Bluelick without the whole town knowing.

Her behavior confirmed what he'd already suspected. She'd heard the same stupid rumor about why Roger and Melody broke up, and decided to turn herself into Roger's perfect nymphomaniac soul mate.

"It's Roger, isn't it?"

She turned to him. "Hmm?"

"He's the reason for our lessons. You heard the rumor about why he and Melody called it quits, and you're trying to become the kind of woman he's looking for."

"That's ridiculous," she said, and took a gulp of her Cabernet.

The not-quite denial sprung to her lips too quickly, and her cheeks turned the same shade as her wine. He sat back and vented a humorless laugh.

"What's so funny?"

"Boy, are you barking up the wrong tree, Doc."

"Are you suggesting he's out of my league?"

And now he sounded like an asshole instead of just feeling like one. Before he could take back the unintended insult and explain what he'd really meant, she leaned in close and spoke in a low voice. "That's what you're implying, isn't it? Because he comes from a good home, with parents who love him and are proud of him, and I—I'm dorky Ellie Swann, with no mother, and a father who can't stand the sight of her—"

"No." He cut her off with the single word and what he hoped was a steady, unflinching look. "No," he repeated, and took her hand. "That's not at all what I'm saying. It's got nothing to do with you. Ellie, didn't you notice which room Roger and his...and Doug, were coming out of...no pun intended?"

"I don't know what you're talking about." She gave her hand a tug. He held on and searched her face. Holy crap, she really didn't have a clue. She honestly hadn't realized they were *together*, not merely shopping together. Hell, they'd been browsing in the "Hard-y Boys" room.

He didn't care to out anybody, but it was on the tip of his tongue to say, "Honey, Roger's gay." He opened his mouth to speak the words, but they refused to come. As soon as she knew, she'd have no need to schedule the rest of their lessons. He'd be a fool to take away her sole reason for being with him.

Talk about irony. After dedicating years to the art of the brief, casual affair, he'd finally found a woman he wanted to spend time with—real time, not just a handful of naked, sweaty hours—and all she wanted from him was sex.

Another realization arrived hot on the heels of the first. It sucked, being the one who wanted more, and he only had five lessons to change her mind.

• • •

Should she apologize to Tyler for getting all defensive at dinner? Ellie stared out the car window at the dark countryside and pondered the question. Probably, yes, considering she'd let her insecurities get the better of her. She'd accused him of thinking Roger was too good for her, even though she knew Tyler wasn't the type to judge people by factors over which they had no control, like their pedigree.

He clearly didn't see her as the ideal woman for Roger, and that hurt. His viewpoint shouldn't have mattered, but rightly or wrongly his opinion had become important to her. She probably ought to get used to surprised, skeptical reactions. Roger and Melody had been Bluelick's "it" couple for eons. Everyone naturally expected the new woman in his life to fit the Melody mold—and she so didn't.

Whether Tyler's reasons for rejecting the possibility that Roger might be interested in her romantically hinged on those factors, she didn't know, because when she'd asked him to explain himself, he'd pokered up and deflected her questions with nonanswers.

She crossed her arms, slumped in her seat, and stared at the moon. Leave it to a man to think that "I'm just saying he's not the guy for you—end of story" constituted a crystal clear response. On the drive home he'd kept his silence to the point she found it daunting. Now, as he took the Bluelick exit, she worried he *was* mad at her for her outburst at dinner. Perhaps mad enough to cancel their lessons?

The thought had her straightening and chewing her lip. She glanced at his profile in the darkened interior of the car. He didn't look perturbed. In fact, he looked a thousand miles away, completely lost in his own thoughts, which probably had nothing to do with her. Mustering her nerve, she said, "Tyler?"

He looked over at her, one brow lifted in the silent, inquiring gesture she found inexplicably appealing.

"I'm sorry I snapped at you during dinner. I guess I'm a little bit defensive about certain things, but I shouldn't have taken it out on you."

He smiled and squeezed her hand. "Don't worry about it, Doc." Apparently finding her hand cold, he moved it to his thigh and trapped it there beneath his palm. Heat seeped through his jeans, warming her fingers—and every erogenous zone in her body.

"Thanks," she managed, shifting slightly in her seat while he cruised down Main Street. He shot her a knowing look and slid their hands a little higher on his leg.

She cleared her throat and pressed her luck. "So, are we on for Friday night?"

"Why wait that long? My place, Thursday night, around seven?"

"I'll be there."

He squeezed her hand and then, much to her disappointment, let go in order to maneuver the car into a curbside slot in front of her office. "In the meantime…" He killed the engine, reached down and released his seat belt, then hers, and pulled her into a slow, deep, take-no-prisoners kiss that made her head spin. She was trying to climb over the center console by the time they broke apart. He rested his forehead against hers and smiled down at her. "That'll have to hold us over 'til Thursday." Next thing she knew, he opened the driver's-side door and stepped out.

She blinked at the now-empty seat opposite her and struggled to retrieve her scattered thoughts. What was she doing, making out in her car like some hormonal teenager, parked directly under a streetlight in the middle of town, where God and everyone could see? It was only half past eight on a beautiful early-summer evening. Plenty of people were still strolling about, enjoying the break in humidity, and if their eyes were sharp, catching Dr. Swann conducting a tonsil exam on Tyler Longfoot with nothing but her tongue. Obviously, she'd lost her mind.

Tyler opened her door and offered her a hand to help her out. She took his hand and stepped out onto the sidewalk on unsteady legs, which she attributed to his hot kiss and cool manners. He gave her the car keys.

"Want me to follow you home?"

"Um, no. That's not necessary. I'm going to get a few things from my office before I head home."

"Okay, then." He leaned in close, until his mouth hovered mere inches above hers. Concerns about witnesses faded from her mind and she parted her lips in anticipation of another mind-altering kiss.

But it didn't come. Instead he smiled his slow, sexy smile and danced his fingertips over her cheek. "See you Thursday. I'll keep the accessories."

She stood there, breathing heavy, while he ambled down the sidewalk toward his truck.

Accessories. Belatedly, she realized he'd taken the shopping bag with him. There went her plan to practice securing and unlocking the handcuffs before "date" night. Sighing, she turned and climbed the steps to her office.

The second she walked in the door she knew something

was amiss. Light shone through the opaque privacy glass shuttering the front office from the waiting area. *What the—?* She distinctly remembered turning all the lights off before she left. They didn't keep much cash in the office, but they had some expensive equipment.

Don't jump to conclusions, she warned herself. A Bluelick crime spree typically involved baseball bats and mailboxes, not breaking and entering. Maybe the cleaning service had left a light on?

Almost as soon as that comforting thought crossed her mind, a muffled but distinctly female cry sounded from the back of the suite, followed by a low, authoritative voice issuing an indistinct command.

Good God, not only did she have an intruder, he was victimizing some helpless woman! She tunneled her trembling hands into her purse, found her phone, and dialed 9-1-1. The call immediately went to hold and she almost burst into tears. The woman cried out again, louder this time and even more desperate. Ellie knew she couldn't just stand in the waiting room while the poor woman suffered. She had to *do* something.

The waiting room door stood ajar. She forced her leaden limbs into motion and pushed it open. The hinges squeaked. She held her breath, listening for any sign that the intruder had heard the noise, but she really couldn't hear much above the sound of her own blood rushing in her ears. Finally, drawing a deep breath, she hugged the wall and inched toward the back of the suite.

Light shone from around the door of the small exam room at the end of the hall. She stopped in the front office area, placed her purse on the counter, and slid the envelope opener from its caddy. Phone in one hand and the makeshift weapon in the other, she crept toward the exam room.

The door wasn't quite closed, and the woman's frenzied

"Oh, God please. Don't! Stop!" carried all too well. Ellie rushed forward, but just as she prepared to burst through the door and surprise the assailant, the slap of a palm connecting with vulnerable flesh reverberated like a shotgun blast. The woman's gasp followed, and then the maniac's chillingly deep, controlled voice.

He sounded big. Powerful. Her best hope was to sneak in silently and pray to go unnoticed until she had the point of her letter opener pressed to the guy's jugular.

Sweat dampened her palms. She tightened her grip on the letter opener, took another deep breath, and slowly... *carefully*...pushed the door open. Using it at as shield, she looked inside the room—and froze.

Melody, of all people, knelt on the exam table, completely naked. A rubber tourniquet banded her wrists. Her knees balanced on the very edge of the padded table and—oh my—Fire Chief Bradley sat on the stool behind her, wearing nothing but his wristwatch and an impressive erection, his face buried between her thighs.

Melody hadn't been pleading "Don't!" and "Stop!" She'd been screaming, "*Don't stop!*"

Paralyzed, Ellie nonetheless noted the inventive twist on chapter 3, combined with certain elements from chapter 6. While she watched, Melody squirmed and begged, and Chief Bradley delivered another playful slap to her round, pink backside. Then he stood, wrapped an arm around Melody's waist, and guided them eagerly into chapter 10. The sound of their mutual, highly enthusiastic endorsement shocked Ellie out of her trance. She did a quick about-face and scurried back the way she'd come.

She'd stupidly assumed running into Roger at the Slap & Tickle would be the most embarrassing thing to happen to her tonight, but after she'd taken two steps toward a silent, undetected exit, a tinny, disembodied voice rang out clear as day. "This is 9-1-1. What is your emergency?"

Utter silence pulsed for a full ten seconds, followed by Melody's "Oh, shit!" and some frenzied rustling.

Ellie kicked her retreat into high gear. "Sorry, false alarm," she whispered into her phone and disconnected. She retrieved her purse and covered the distance to her car in record time—for a short-strided nonathlete wearing heels and a tight skirt. Still, not quite fast enough, unfortunately, because as she revved the engine and prepared to drive away, she saw lights come on in the waiting room and the slats of the lowered blinds part to give someone a view of the street. Busted. Melody would recognize her silver Mini.

Then again, maybe Melody and Chief Bradley were the busted ones? She peeled away from the curb, fighting a highly inappropriate urge to giggle. She lost. Her giggles turned to outright laughter, which only escalated as adrenaline retreated, leaving her limp and giddy with relief. Laughing helplessly at the absurdity of walking in on her office manager having wild, acrobatic sex with the new fire chief, she tried to guess which of them was the most mortified—Melody, Chief Bradley, or her. Hard to say.

Her giggles died in her throat when she considered the possibility Melody might quit, out of embarrassment or outrage. God knows she hadn't meant to do it, but she'd basically spied on them having sex. Why, why, why couldn't she have managed a silent, anonymous exit from the office? She'd spent the better part of twenty-eight years garnering minimal notice from her own father. Being invisible should be second nature to her.

It wasn't until the pretty white pickets of her front porch filled her windshield that an even more disquieting thought occurred to her. Melody had seemed comfortable—make that blissfully happy—performing variations on chapters 3, 6, and 10. She certainly hadn't appeared the least bit uptight or

inhibited. Yet she and Roger had split because she'd declined
to match his sexual adventurousness.

So what the hell chapter was Roger on?

• • •

"I guess we know each other's deepest secrets now," a low
voice whispered over Ellie's shoulder, snapping her out of her
sleep-deprived fugue and into reality, which at the moment
consisted of standing in Jiffy Java, awaiting her iced double
espresso. *Roger.* A slight smile curved his sculpted lips, but
the shadows under his eyes suggested he hadn't slept any
better than she had.

"Um...you mean our preference for shopping in
Lexington?" After everything she'd witnessed yesterday
evening, she vowed to assume nothing.

He nodded and leaned closer, until she could smell the
mint of his toothpaste. "Yeah. Running into you in Lexington
was completely unexpected. I'm sure you figured out I
wasn't there buying stuff for a party. We should probably get
together and talk. In private. If you're free tonight I could
make dinner for us at my place?"

Holy smokes, Roger wanted to have dinner with her!
Things were suddenly progressing. *Too fast*, a voice in her
head protested. She wasn't ready. Especially not after what
she'd seen last night of Melody's talents.

She couldn't possibly spend an evening alone with Roger
until she'd at least mastered chapters 3 and 6 and a wild
card—ideally, chapter 13—assuming she could talk Tyler
into it. Strangely, while the thought of attempting any or all
the lessons with Tyler sent bone-melting heat all the way to
her toes, the notion of trying any of the *Wild Woman* tactics
on Roger caused her insides to twist painfully. Anxiety, she
surmised. Tyler made sex fun and exciting. She didn't have to

pretend to be a talented, worldly woman. Roger, on the other hand, sought an inventive, experienced partner.

"I can't tonight. How about…" *Buy some time!* "…later this weekend?"

He shook his head. "I leave early Friday for a weekend getaway. A friend and I are headed to Miami. How about dinner Monday after I get back?"

Perfect. Several days to work on her skills and her nerve. "Monday works. Since you'll be fresh from vacation, I'll make dinner at my place." She hoped her smile didn't look as stiff as it felt.

He smiled back, looking a little stiff, too. "In the meantime, I'd really appreciate it if you wouldn't discuss… um…you know…what you saw in Lexington."

"Of course not." Spotting her drink on the counter, she reached out to retrieve it. "I won't tell a soul I spotted Bluelick's newest lawyer at Slap & Tickle if you won't tell anyone you saw the town doctor there."

He tapped his to-go cup against hers. "You got yourself a deal, Sparky. I'll see you Monday."

My plan is finally coming together, she thought as she crossed the town square on the way to her office. Neither the caffeine nor the smell of southern magnolias bordering the square accounted for her improved energy. A date with Roger charged her system better than aromatherapy or a double espresso. She was so preoccupied planning what she'd say to him when they were finally alone and able to speak freely, she completely forgot the other reason for her restless night.

Forgot, that is, until she walked through the front door of her office and nearly tripped over Melody, who was arranging the magazines on the waiting room end table closest to the door. The blonde immediately straightened and smoothed her hands down the skirt of her peach-printed sundress.

"Hi, Ellie. Sorry, I know I'm early." She glanced around the waiting room, as if not sure where to let her gaze rest, then looked at Ellie, swallowed and continued. "I aimed to get here early in case you wanted to…you know"—she looked away again and smiled thinly—"fire me."

"Oh, God no." She clamped a hand on Melody's arm. "I was afraid you were going to quit."

Melody shook her head. "I love this job. I don't want to lose it." She closed her eyes and cringed. "I can't believe I did something so crazy and unprofessional."

"Um, wasn't it you who walked in on Tyler and me kissing in exam room one a few weeks ago? I'd be kind of a hypocrite, calling *you* unprofessional."

"This was worse. I don't know what I was thinking. Actually, that's not true. I was thinking it had been so *damn* long since a gorgeous, sexy, incredibly attentive guy literally wanted to tear my clothes off and have his merry way with me. And then I just completely stopped thinking."

"Who could blame you?" Ellie quickly reassured her, all the while wondering why Roger didn't qualify. Pushing the question aside, she added, "Not any healthy, red-blooded woman in the county between the ages of eighteen and eighty, because I hear there's been a suspicious uptick in small kitchen fires since Chief Bradley landed in Bluelick."

A smile pulled at the corners of Melody's mouth before she turned and led the way through the waiting room and into the front office area, stopping at the counter where the day's charts were already racked. "I really am sorry, and mortified, and I promise, nothing like last night will ever happen again."

"Hey, for your sake, I hope it happens all the time, just not anyplace where a bonehead like me will bumble along."

"Oh, you're not a bonehead. I'm sure you were terrified, and then horrified."

"Try surprised, and then relieved. Honestly, Melody,

don't give the incident another thought. I know you didn't plan it."

"I didn't. I hadn't even planned on seeing Josh last night, much less getting naked with the man. But I ran into him at Boone's Market and it felt so good, talking with him, feeling that zing of attraction when he looked at me, realizing he felt the same chemistry. When he invited me to take a tour of the firehouse, I knew we were both looking for an excuse to spend more time together. But the firehouse is a busy place, full of other firefighters and what have you, so afterward, I offered to take him on a tour of my workplace. As soon as we were alone, things just sort of ignited. I really am sorry. Josh is, too."

"Don't worry about it." She started to turn toward her office, then stopped and looked at Melody. "So...are you going to see Chief Bradley again?"

"You've seen him as naked as a newborn, Ellie. I think under the circumstances, you should call him Josh."

"You're evading the question, Miss Merritt."

"Yes," she said softly. "He asked me to dinner Friday night. I accepted before I could talk myself out of it."

"Why would you want to talk yourself out of it?"

"Please. I've got 'woman in transition' written all over me, and I know it. I'm coming off a long-term relationship and a broken engagement. My head's telling me stuff like, 'Take things slow. Have fun. Don't dive into anything serious.'"

"Sounds logical."

"Yeah. Too bad my heart took one look at Josh and said, 'Mine, mine, mine!'"

"It's a little-known medical fact. The heart's got a mind of its own. I guess yours is over Roger, then?"

The overhead lights bounced off Melody's shimmering tresses as she nodded. "For a long time. We'd drifted into friendship well before we called our engagement off. It just took us a while to admit as much to each other."

Ellie weighed her options. She was beginning to think of Melody as a friend, but what did the rules of friendship dictate in this situation? Should she give Melody a heads-up before dating her ex? Ellie's conscience said yes.

"Okay, well, the thing is…" She took a deep, fortifying breath. "Roger and I are going on a date when he gets back from vacation."

Her statement hung in the air. Melody's eyes widened and her eyebrows almost disappeared into her hairline. "Roger asked you out?"

Melody didn't sound angry so much as shocked. Crap. She shouldn't have said anything.

"He did. We're having dinner at my place." Deciding honesty was the best policy, she went on. "I've always liked Roger. In school, I had a big crush on him. Now that we're both back in Bluelick, I realize my crush never completely faded, but maybe evolved into something new. I think he sees me in a new light, too."

As Ellie watched, Melody's peaches-and-cream complexion turned a fierce shade of red. "You're mad," Ellie said.

"Not with you, no. But I'm mad as hell at him because— because—" She closed her eyes and took a slow, measured breath before continuing. "I can't even tell you why I'm upset, because I can't think of a way to explain without breaking a promise. But it's not because I'm some crazy, jealous ex." She rubbed a hand over her forehead and stared hard at the wall, obviously weighing her words. "I don't want to see somebody else's time wasted."

Did Melody assume she'd run for the hills as soon as she found out Roger liked to get kinky?

She cleared her throat and stared her very own hole through the wall. "I…ah…I know what I'm getting into."

The door to the waiting room opened. Sweet little old Ms. Van Hendler, the first patient of the day, toddled in and approached the window.

Melody gave Ellie a strained look and handed her the chart. "I know you think you do, but you don't. I know I'm not making any sense. Just remember, I'm here for you."

"What was that, dear?" Ms. Van Hendler piped in.

Melody smiled, "I said, 'Ms. Van Hendler, we're clear for you.' Come on back." With that, she got up to show the patient into the exam room.

Ellie released a pent-up breath and fanned her flaming face with the chart. *That went well.*

Chapter Twelve

"Ready, Doc?" Tyler asked, and tossed her onto his bed. He liked the way she looked, lying across his sheets in nothing but a red satin bra and some very small matching panties. When she smiled and nodded, he wrapped a hand around her ankle and started kissing his way to chapter 3. Hopefully they'd get all the way through this time.

He didn't get far before she tugged her foot away and sat up. "Wait. What are you doing?"

Although he knew damn well what she was getting at, he couldn't resist teasing. "Doc, if you have to ask, you probably ought to study that guide of yours again." He made a grab for her ankle. She twisted like an eel and scrambled off the bed.

"You've got this backward again. I'm supposed to do you. Tyler, you *promised* you'd let me take the lead."

He sighed and lowered himself to the mattress. "I said I'd try."

"Well, try harder."

"Okay, fine." He settled back against his sturdy, hand-hewn oak headboard. "It's your show."

"Good."

Lord, she was adorable, standing there in scraps of red satin, hair tousled, looking like she'd just won a wrestling match. But then her victory smile slipped some.

"Problem?"

Her brow knitted, she bit her lip, and it took every ounce of willpower he possessed not to yank her back down of the bed, crush those pouty lips to his, and take charge until they were both begging for mercy.

"Yes. According to the illustration in my book, you're supposed to sit here." She pointed to the edge of the bed.

"Where are you going to be?"

"I'll be down here, on the floor." She knelt beside the bed.

The button fly of his jeans turned into a torture device at the sight, but he couldn't help playing with her a little more. "Seems needlessly uncomfortable for you. The bed is plenty big." Parting his legs, he patted the mattress between them invitingly.

She considered his proposal for a moment, chewing her lip the whole time, and slowly shook her head. "No. I think we should stick to the book."

"Okay." He assumed the preferred position and gave her a quick squeeze with his knees. "But for a wild woman, you're awfully strict on the logistics." His amusement dried up when she rested her hands on his thighs.

"Wild woman in training," she corrected, and reached for his fly.

He intercepted her hand. "Just hold on a minute. This book of yours says just sit the guy down, whip it out, and get to work?"

She frowned and he could practically hear the gears in her mind turning while she mentally reviewed everything she'd read. "Um, I guess they didn't really cover any particular lead-in. Is there something I'm supposed to do first?"

"You could try touching me."

"Where?"

"Anywhere you want. Gently," he added when her eyes zoomed in on his crotch.

She nodded and, to his surprise, placed her hands on his knees. Slowly, she ran them up his thighs, following the inseams of his jeans. He held his breath when she reached the top, then expelled it slowly as she trailed her hands down again.

"Wasn't so tough, was it?"

Her eyes flicked to his. "No. To be honest, I've got kind of a thing about your legs." Her hands started up again, this time her thumbs leading the way. His cock began throb impatiently.

"That so?" The words scraped over his throat like sandpaper.

"Umm-hmm. They're long and muscular. I've been wondering if those muscles felt as good as they look." Having reached the top of his inseam, she shifted her hands around to the front of his thighs and squeezed. "They do."

Holy shit, he was going to die.

"Anything else you've been wondering about?"

Nodding, she scooted closer, grabbed the hem of his T-shirt, and gave it a little tug. Obligingly, he lifted his arms and she swept it over his head. After tossing the shirt away, her eyes found his. She rested her hands on his pecs and just stared at him for a long moment. Then her eyes dropped and her breath shuddered out in a rush.

"Good lord, Tyler, you're like a work of art."

The reverence in her voice sent heat creeping up his neck. "I've been called a lot of things, Doc, but never art."

"Well, it's true," she insisted, and slid her palms down his chest and along his stomach. She stopped there, her hands moving restlessly back and forth over his painfully tight abs.

"What happened here?" she asked, fingers tracing the pale scar slashed down his side. "Another wild night at Rawley's?"

The scar was a souvenir from Big Joe, but he wasn't about to bring his dearly departed daddy into the evening. "No, it's old…"

His explanation ended in a groan when she lowered her head and ran her lips along the jagged line. He buried his hand in her hair and dragged her head up for a long, hot kiss. When he eased back, she pressed her forehead against the underside of his jaw and inhaled slowly.

"Anything else you want to touch, Doc?"

Her eyes dropped to his lap. "Now?"

"Now would be awesome."

She slipped one hand into the front of his jeans, nails scraping lightly under the waistband of his shorts on her quest to find him. He surged up to meet those roving fingers and suddenly, circulation became a critical thing. Groaning, he tugged at his fly. Like a homing pigeon, her free hand followed and their fingers tangled in a frantic race to pop the buttons. Finally, they had his jeans open, his shorts shoved down, and her hand banded around his brutally sensitive cock.

He watched, halfway between amused and agonized, as she looked down and sucked in a breath.

"I'd forgotten all about *your* nickname until now."

He laughed, even though her busy hands were fast eliminating his ability to think straight. "What nickname?"

"Footlong Longfoot."

"And here I thought people were talking about my feet."

She laughed, as he'd hoped, and ran her hand slowly, tentatively up his shaft. Figuring a teacher's job was to teach, he covered her hand with his and showed her how he liked to be touched. His attentive student followed his lead. After a minute of sheer heaven, she spoke up.

"Tyler, I think my experts might have assumed, ah, smaller dimensions when they wrote chapter 3. I'm not sure I can do this exactly as they instructed."

"What you're doing right now works fine—"

Before he realized her intent, she ducked her head and kissed the tip of his dick.

"Well, okay, then…that works, too…"

Parting her lips just enough to take him in, keeping the seal tight, she inched lower…and lower.

His eyelids drooped to half-mast and his vision went blurry. "More," he begged, even though she was probably approaching the most she could take. He swept his thumb lightly along her jaw and, God bless her, she took more. When she hummed deep in her throat and retraced her path, he felt the vibrations all the way to the soles of his feet. It took considerable effort not to whimper.

Maybe he did whimper, because she lifted her head and looked at him. "Was that okay?"

Somehow found his voice. "Ellie, you do that to any man, he's going to be promising you diamond earrings…a weekend in Paris…whatever you want."

She smiled and lowered her head again, and it was just as amazing the second time, but now, thanks to his comment, he had the thought of her doing the very same thing to some other guy stuck in his head. Not just stuck there, but *messing* with it. Suddenly, he hated the idea of being her tutor, her guinea pig, her stepping-stone to something bigger and better. With a vague, restless determination to show her he was the biggest and best, he pulled her up and tossed her onto the bed.

She landed on her back and immediately sat up. "Hey! I wasn't done yet—"

"You've got the gist of chapter 3," he ground out as he kicked off his jeans and shorts. "Consider this a two-fer."

• • •

"A two-fer?" Ellie repeated and watched him close in on her. "What does that mean?" She wished she knew why being manhandled by Tyler made her weak in the knees, but Lord help her, it did. It really did. But when he started to drag her panties down, another thought occurred to her.

"Hold on." She scooted out of his grasp.

"What's wrong?"

"Nothing's wrong. It's just that plain old missionary style isn't one of the lessons I bookmarked. I've done missionary before."

He looked at her for a full second, his expression unreadable. "Chapter 10," he growled, and in a heart-stopping move, flipped her over. With a strong arm under her hips, he hauled her onto her knees and elbows. The suddenness of his actions jostled a squeak from her throat.

"Shh," he whispered and smoothed his wide palm over her hip, mistaking her reaction for nervousness. "We'll take it slow."

At this point, as far as she was concerned, he could take it any way he damn well pleased, so long as he took, but still she couldn't help mentioning, "You're going out of order."

He reached beyond her and snagged a small packet from his nightstand. Her insides trembled.

"News flash, Doc. Order's overrated. Besides, you've spent enough time staring at my ass. Seems past time I returned the favor."

With that, he tore her panties off. She gasped, but when his tongue took a long, unhurried slide down her spine, all the way to the small of her back, the gasp edged over into a moan. He kissed a line across the top of one bare cheek, then the other. Meanwhile his fingers delved between her legs, stroking, teasing…forcing her breath to come in ragged pants.

"Tyler...please."

"I *am* here to please," he whispered against her skin. "Tell me what you want."

"You. Inside me. Now."

"At your service," he said with such playful tenderness she didn't know whether to laugh or burst into tears. Then she felt the hot, heavy length of him slide down her backside and all she wanted to do was hurry. She couldn't help arching and lifting to help him along any more than she could bite back a low, needy cry when he insinuated himself between her thighs—a cry that merged with his groan of pleasure when he nudged forward until he just barely penetrated her.

"Oh, God. Hurry," she managed.

He kissed her shoulder, her neck. His voice rumbled in her ear, "Slow and steady."

Slow and steady? She couldn't afford slow or steady... she'd lose her mind in another thirty seconds if he didn't do something to assuage the ache building to an unbearably sweet crisis. She pushed backward, trying to take him deeper.

Hands on her hips held her still. "I'm the boss, remember?"

"Tutor," she panted.

"Whatever."

She concentrated on breathing while he did his slow and steady thing, using controlled thrusts to ease himself in. Braced on one arm, he swept his hand over her breast, cupping the underside, tormenting her nipple until she moaned. The need building where their bodies joined was so big, so consuming, she couldn't think beyond it.

"Jesus, you feel good. Hot and tight." His fingers glided between her thighs. "Wet."

She couldn't have held still if her life depended on it. Forehead pressed to the pillow, she moved her hips in a shallow, rocking motion, the best she could do with the backstop of his body pressed so tight to hers.

He wouldn't be rushed, just wrapped his arm around her waist and continued to move slowly, stretch her slowly, fill her slowly, until she thought she'd die from pleasure. Finally, when he was buried deep and she could feel every hot, pulsing inch of him inside her, he whispered, "You ready, Ellie?"

Her body clenched around him in answer.

With a rough groan, he drove into her, unleashing a series of fast, powerful thrusts that rocketed her right to the gates of heaven. The rhythmic slap of their bodies echoed in her ears while she knelt there, sheets bunched in her fists, face buried in the pillow, control and dignity somewhere far beyond her reach and she didn't give a damn because ecstasy shimmered so incredibly close. Frantic for release, she bucked and strained, and bit back a sob because try as she might, she couldn't quite get there.

Tyler made a sympathetic sound and skimmed his fingers down between her legs again. Incoherent with gratitude, she pressed herself into his helping hand. Then he thumbed the unbearably sensitive trigger that shot her headlong into a sweet, sweeping oblivion. She cried out and lost herself in the free fall.

• • •

Minutes, or hours, later, she shook herself out of a pleasure-induced stupor and took inventory. She lay naked across blissfully cool sheets in something very close to a boneless puddle. Warm, nimble lips nibbled their way along her shoulder while talented fingertips traced curlicues down her spine. When they moved on to her butt, she forced her eyes open and found herself adrift in Tyler's clear green gaze.

Why couldn't all her relationships be this easy? Her situation with Frank was fraught with unresolved, and possibly unresolvable, issues. She hadn't maintained anything close to a simple employer-employee relationship with Melody. But this thing with Tyler worked perfectly.

Aglow with the foolproof simplicity of their arrangement, she smiled at him.

"Doc, which complete moron from your past convinced you your bedroom skills needed work?"

She blew out a breath and her happy glow dimmed a little because she couldn't be completely honest with him about her motives. "It's not like that. I mean, nobody complained. I just felt like I needed to push myself out of my comfort zone, so to speak." To avoid his inevitable "why," she rushed on. "Haven't you ever felt like you needed to change in order to make your dreams come true?"

He rolled onto his back and stared at the ceiling, forearm resting across his forehead. "Yeah, just lately. I think that was the bank's message to me, in a nutshell. Want a loan on the Browning place? Start behaving like a responsible, grown-ass man."

"They're off base in their assessment."

One corner of his mouth lifted in a half smile. "Nah, they've got some valid points. I tend to please myself, do things my own way, and I don't worry overly much about the future. These traits make me a reliability risk in the bank's eyes. They want to see some investment *from* me—in my business and my life—before they make one *in* me."

Ellie propped her chin in her hand and stared at his entrancing profile. "Well, I still say they're not looking very hard at what you bring to Bluelick. You operate your business here and provide jobs in this community. That's an investment. The volunteer work you do also qualifies as an investment."

Tyler reached over and pulled her across his chest. "You tell 'em, Sparky."

"I'm serious," she puffed, shoving her hair out of her face.

"I know you are." His grin disappeared. He took her hand and placed a soft kiss on her wrist. "I appreciate your opinion. It matters to me." While her heart tripped and words tangled in her throat, his sly grin reappeared. "Junior and I are re-presenting our case to the lending committee Tuesday. Want to be a character reference? Tell them how reliable I am? How thoroughly I get the job done?"

She tried but failed to hold back a laugh. "I'm not sure I'm qualified, seeing as how I only have a lesson and a half to go by—"

"*A half*?" He lifted his head and stared at her, green eyes flashing. "Where the hell are you getting a half? That was two full lessons, no matter how you're counting."

"Okay, okay, two lessons. And the truth is, they have been incredibly educational. I didn't have the first clue what I was doing before. Thanks to you I finally understand what all the fuss is about. Who knows? I might actually be able to impress someone next time around."

He dropped his head back to the pillow and stared at the ceiling. "Glad to help you make a good impression, Doc."

But he didn't sound glad. He sounded pissed. She wasn't sure where she'd gone wrong in her attempt to convey her gratitude, but she rushed to undo the error. The last thing she wanted to do was offend him, especially when she hoped to talk him into fast-tracking their lessons. "I'm sorry. Can I delete what I said and replace it with 'thank you'?"

He sighed and stared back at her, brooding eyes scanning her face. "Yeah, if I can do the same. You spelled out what you wanted from this arrangement right from the start, and I agreed. I don't know what crawled up my ass for a second." Reaching out, he swept her hair away from her forehead. "The heat, I guess…"

A depressing thought snuck into her brain, and flew out

of her mouth before she could edit it. "You're probably feeling stuck—trapped in this deal with me for another three weeks."

He gave her hair a light pull, but his eyes stayed serious. "That's not it."

"Nice of you to say, but I know spending weeks and weeks with the same girl isn't your style. Long-term commitments make you nervous. I understand."

When he opened his mouth to interrupt, she rushed on. "We could tighten the lesson schedule if you have the flexibility, and finish by the end of the week. I'm thinking chapter 6 tomorrow, then the last two chapters Saturday and Sunday. That way you can see a light at the end of the tunnel."

An empty ache swelled in her chest at the thought of their lessons coming to an end. Spending time with him had quickly become the best part of her week. True, as a sex tutor, he proved exasperating, bossy, and...unmanageable at times, but also flat-out fun and easy to talk to. She'd never been so completely herself with anyone, ever. Even with her closest friends from med school, she kept parts of her life hidden from view—mostly the Frank parts—because revealing them left her feeling too vulnerable and pathetic. Tyler somehow saw those parts without her saying a word, which should have made her wary of him. But he didn't mouth platitudes or try to deny the obvious. He simply understood, and by understanding, lightened some of the weight. No wonder she yearned for more.

Don't go there, her mind warned. "More" with Tyler wasn't in the plans—his or hers. He wasn't looking to fall in love, settle down, and start a family. Heck, it was all he could do to curb his wild ways long enough to appease the savings and loan. She and Tyler simply didn't share the same goals, but even if they did, there couldn't be two people less qualified to attain those goals together. Now, Roger, on the other hand—

"I'm not looking for a light at the end of the tunnel, Ellie," Tyler said quietly, cutting into her thoughts. "But we can take the lessons at whatever pace you want. I'm free tomorrow night. Pencil me in for chapter 6."

Chapter Thirteen

Ellie knelt on her bed and watched, heart pounding, as Tyler dug into the Slap & Tickle bag on her nightstand and withdrew the handcuffs, but when she reached for them, he raised an eyebrow and lifted them out of her grasp. "You've got the scenario turned around, Doc. You're the helpless hostage. I'm your merciless captor."

For a moment, all she could do was stare at him. Was he serious? Every fantasy she'd hatched about chapter 6 involved tying him up and taking advantage of him. The opposite scenario never entered her mind.

"No, no." She grabbed the *Wild Woman* guide from her nightstand. "According to the book, you're the one who wears the cuffs and the blindfold."

"I don't think so." Intercepting, he opened the book to chapter 6, turned it around so she could see, and tapped the illustration. "This figure here, with the long hair and the breasts, blindfolded and tied to the bed? That's you. The one straddling her, with the penis? That would be me."

"You can't just go by the picture." She took the book from

him. "If you'd read the chapter, you'd know the illustration is just that, an example. You have to determine which person in the couple is the dominant and which the submissive, in terms of sexual personality."

Instead of conceding to her superior research, he shrugged and started working her plum-colored satin panties down her legs. "Right. So let's get rid of these, and then you reach on up there and grab the rails. I'll cuff you and—"

"*I'm* not the submissive one in our duo."

"Honey," he said, half-indulgent, half-amused, as if she'd just insisted she could beat him arm-wrestling.

"Don't 'honey' me. I'm serious."

"Not three days ago you accused me of always having to be in control, and now I'm the submissive?"

"You're a textbook case. Look," she ran a finger across the page until she found the paragraph she sought. "It says right here, 'Don't pigeonhole your alpha stud as the dominant in your sexual scenarios.'" She slapped her free hand against his chest to hold him back when he closed in with the cuffs. "'Though perhaps counterintuitive, a physically powerful man may find more pleasure in the submissive role, precisely because he perceives the alternative dynamic—dominating a smaller, weaker woman—inequitable.'"

"You saying I'm too much of a gentleman to tie you up?"

"Not me. The experts."

"Here's what I think of your experts." In a domineering move that might have melted her panties had she been wearing any, he clasped her wrists in one big hand. Before she could even think about protesting, her arms were stretched above her head, secured in handcuffs wrapped around the center rail of her brass headboard.

He leaned back and admired his handiwork. "I defy all your experts."

Lying nearly naked before him, wearing only a lacy bra

and handcuffs, she wondered if he had a point. Then she tested the cuffs. "You did it wrong, Longfoot. These are way too loose. If I wanted to, I could slide right out."

. "I'm not holding you against your will." He tugged his T-shirt over his head, subjecting her to a fascinating play of light over the muscled terrain of his torso. "If I'm doing my job right"—he tossed the shirt aside—"you won't want to slide out."

Not want her hands free to tear his jeans off? Not want to touch him all over? Not likely. And this was exactly why he wasn't the dominant. He'd happily charm her pants off, didn't mind the occasional show of strength, but he'd never overpower and *take*. Such antics violated his personal code, even as a game.

She didn't suffer the same compunction. "Kiss me," she ordered, then bided her time as he leaned in and delivered on her request. When his mouth fused to hers and their tongues embarked on a slippery duel for supremacy, she slithered out of the cuffs. Taking full advantage of the element of surprise, she reared up, twisted, and rolled until he lay flat on his back and she straddled his chest. Then she cuffed his wrists around the headboard.

"You out to prove something, Sparky?" His teasing smile dimmed only slightly when he tried to pull his hands free and found them secured snugly. No sliding out for him.

"That's Mistress Ellie to you." She reached for the blindfold he'd placed on the nightstand, bringing her lace-covered breasts enticingly close to his mouth in the process.

"Hmm. Come here, Mistress Ellie."

She tortured them both by dangling one breast close enough that he could, and did, run his tongue over the nipple visibly straining against the wispy barrier.

"Closer," he demanded, flicking his tongue over her again.

"Closer, *please*, Mistress Ellie," she corrected, unable to stifle a smirk, even as her nipple tightened and ached to feel his lips.

Predictably, he read her body's reaction. Instead of giving her what she craved, he relaxed against the pillow with a slow, confident smile. "Take off these handcuffs, and I'll lick a hell of a lot more than one nipple."

Arching her brows at him, she picked up the blindfold, ran it leisurely through her hand, and then pulled it taut. "Don't tell Mistress Ellie what to do."

"If Mistress Ellie puts that blindfold on me, it's going to be a damn long time before those pretty little breasts get the attention they're begging for."

"Mistress Ellie doesn't appreciate threats," she replied in her strictest voice, and attempted to tie the blindfold on him even as he made a move to evade.

"Ow! Jesus, why not yank all the hair out of my scalp?"

Oops. She untied the knot and started again. "If you'd be still for one lousy second—"

A long-suffering sigh signaled his capitulation. "Doc, I can't tell you what a turn-on this is."

With the blindfold in place, she unceremoniously pressed the heel of her hand against his forehead and shoved him back against the pillow. Then she scooted down until she straddled his hips. That's when she discovered, despite his complaints, he wasn't completely turned off.

Pausing a moment, she sat back to appreciate the sight of him all bound and shirtless and annoyed. He expelled a breath.

She rolled her eyes and released the front clasp of her bra. The small noise filled the room, as did the rustle of fabric when she slid the garment down her arms.

"Okay," he muttered, "that might have been slightly hot." The surge of his erection between her thighs suggested he found it more than just slightly arousing.

Empowered, she leaned forward until the very tips of her breasts made contact with his chest. He sucked in a breath and groaned.

"Shh. No talking." To enforce the rule, she planted a kiss on his unsuspecting mouth. Excitement caused her to slam her lips down on his harder than she'd meant to. He angled his head up and returned the kiss with equal fervor, using his teeth and tongue to turn captor into slave.

Determined to exploit her advantage, she trailed her mouth over his chin and jaw, taking tiny bites as she went. When she moved to his throat, a cautionary "Ellie" rumbled against her lips. Undaunted, she kissed a line from his Adam's apple all the way down to the waistband of his Levi's. He shivered, probably as much from the sensation of her hair tickling his skin as anything she did with her mouth.

Time to bring her hands into play. Again, giving him no tip-off as to her next move— gotta love the blindfold—she cupped him through his jeans.

"Oh, fuck," burst from his lips in a breathless protest, but he dug his heels into the mattress and lifted his hips so he could push himself deeper into her hand. Continuing to cup and rub him with one hand, she undid his fly with the other. The corded muscles in his arms flexed as he gripped the rails of her headboard. His jaw tensed on a groan.

"Enough," he panted. "You've proven your point. I'm turned on. Untie me now."

. . .

Mistress Ellie merely laughed—a low, unrepentant sound— and continued to fondle him while he jumped and twitched in her hand like a puppy eager to be petted. Then his jeans were moving south, her hot mouth closing around him, and clear thought became impossible.

The inability to think didn't stop his mouth from running while she amused herself between his legs. He knew that much, because he could hear his own conflicting words— *God, don't stop, don't ever stop... Christ, stop. You're killing me.* She pretty much ignored what he said and handled him as she saw fit, continuing the sweet torture until he broke his own etiquette rules and indiscriminately thrust his hips in an effort to go deeper.

Again, with no warning whatsoever—Mistress Ellie apparently wasn't a big fan of advance notice—she slid away. "Patience, Tyler," she whispered, then burned a path from his navel to his earlobe with her tongue while a noise he could only describe as a helpless plea emanated from the back of his tight, dry throat.

She caught his earlobe between her teeth and bit. He inhaled sharply and her sweet, evocative scent assailed him. "We've got one more piece of wardrobe to deal with."

God help him, what kind of insanity had her book recommended now? A moment later her got his answer. He didn't know whether to thank her or curse her when she gripped his shaft and rolled a condom on, moving leisurely down his throbbing length, turning the small chore into sweet agony. Before he could recover, she shifted and eased down on him.

A lightning bolt of pleasure singed a path straight from his dick to his brain stem. Light exploded behind his closed eyelids. "Jesus, Ellie," tore from his lips. He was a big guy. She was small and tight. Delicate. He'd never entered her without first ensuring she was good and ready—so ready he could touch and taste it. Tonight he could do neither, but here she was, jumping on without any caution. "Go slow," he directed between clenched teeth, trying to hold himself in check while her body quivered and clenched around him.

The words provoked more laughter, breathless but triumphant. She began to move—up and down, back and forth, deep and fast—and concern for her comfort disappeared, along with everything else except the feel of her. "We've been over this, Tyler," she said. "You don't tell Mistress Ellie what to do. Now I'm going to have to punish you."

Okay, he got advanced warning, but it hardly mattered, because he had no way of knowing her "punishment" would involve cupping his balls and squeezing. Hard. Hard enough to strand him on a thin, sharp precipice halfway between heaven and hell.

"I swear to God, you do that again I'm going to—"

"What?" she challenged, and damn her, squeezed again.

Come, as it turned out. Helplessly, endlessly, in an avalanche of sensation that left him wrung out and shuddering.

"Jesus, Ellie...that was..." She'd drained him so thoroughly, he couldn't finish a sentence. Amazing? Paralyzing? Somewhere between the best and most annihilating experience of his life?

Ellie whisked the blindfold off and smiled down at him with sly, feline superiority. Leaning forward until her mouth brushed his ear, she whispered, "Told you you're the submissive."

He wanted to call bullshit, but when she levered herself up to uncuff him, his exhausted penis slipped out of its favorite place, making him feel even less dominating. Definitely not something he could live with. As soon as his wrists were free, a quick flex of his hips toppled her, and a fast flip put him back on top. Pinning her hands by her head, he inquired, "Now who's the submissive?"

"Brute strength proves nothing."

"Don't you worry, Doc, there's more to me than brute strength."

She raised her eyebrows and ground her hips against

his. "Right now? I don't think so. Male sexual recovery time being what it is, I'd say my dominant status is safe for at least another ten minutes."

He smiled a slow, deliberate smile. "Don't be too sure. I brought a friend."

Those arched brows of hers furrowed into an adorably crinkled line. "A friend?"

"That's right." He reached into the shopping bag and pulled out a neon-pink Bunny. "Say hello to my little friend. I like to call him...Thumper." A quick flick of the power button, and he waved the humming, gyrating vibrator in front of her.

She shrieked and tried to squirm away. Luckily, fast reflexes ran in his blood. She didn't get far, and when he finally introduced Thumper properly, her protests turned to the sweet, breathless cries he knew so well.

"Love that sound," he said and teased the head of the phallus directly over the spot he knew would increase the volume and frequency. "I could listen all night." With that, he moved Thumper to less sensitive territory. Her cries subsided into a low, edgy moan. "All night," he repeated, and retraced the path, delighted to discover she could, when correctly motivated, intersperse those "I'm about to come" cries with some very effective begging.

An hour later, they lay tangled across her bed, limp and panting, and for his part at least, satisfyingly sore in a few key muscle groups. "You can put an A+ next to chapter 6," he mumbled, enjoying the sensation of her fingernails running lightly over his shoulders.

"Thanks. Speaking of my list, I hoped next time we could cover chapter—"

A fist pounding on her front door cut her off. Then a slurred voice yelled, "Ellie! Open the damn door or I'll kick it in. I've had enough of you badmouthing me 'round town."

The fist pounded again. "Open! This! Door!"

Ellie groaned and crossed her arms over her eyes, effectively covering her face. "Go away, Frank," she whispered.

She couldn't possibly know how utterly alone and adrift she looked. Historically, such a look would have served as his cue to get the hell out—and sweep Frank off her doorstep while he was at it—because God knew he didn't have the first clue how to stick around and be somebody's anchor. Have some laughs? Sure. Take on a problem that couldn't be fixed with power tools or sex or both? Not within his skill set. But for some crazy reason, with Ellie, he wanted to dig in and try. Not just because the situation between her and her father brought out every protective instinct he possessed, but because, for once, he wanted to anchor someone...and he wanted someone anchored to him. Another realization rushed up and slapped him in the face on the heels of the first. He'd fallen for her—for her sometimes amusing, sometimes confounding combination of strength, brains, drive, vulnerability, and mile-wide stubborn streak. He'd fallen for the whole complicated package, screwed-up father included.

Frank banged on the door again.

"I'll go have a chat with him," he said, reaching for his jeans. He didn't know how Frank would react to him answering Ellie's door, and he really didn't give a flying fuck. Father or not, the guy was out of line showing up in the middle of the night, yelling and cursing.

"No, don't." She got up and retrieved her robe from the hook on the bathroom door. "Nothing personal, but you going out there will only make things worse. Do me a huge favor and just stay here."

He yanked his jeans up and opened his mouth to tell her even a lap dog wasn't *that* submissive, but then he saw her face—a heartbreaking blend of misery and mortification— and knew whatever he did to insert himself into the situation with Frank would add to her embarrassment. Maybe he shouldn't have cared, because Ellie's pride-saving preferences didn't trump keeping her out of harm's way, but he remembered too well the humiliation of having Big Joe show up somewhere, drunk and on a tear. About now she desperately wanted Frank to shut up and go home, with as few witnesses as possible. He understood.

Because he did, he waited until her big, reluctant eyes met his, and said as gently but firmly as he could manage, "Go tell him I'll be out in a minute to drive him home."

"Tyler, please…stay here."

"Not a chance. I don't know how he got here, but he's not staying, and he sure as hell isn't going anywhere under his own steam in his condition."

"I'll take him home."

"Guess again. You think you can force him into your car if he doesn't want to go?"

She parted her beautiful, kiss-swollen lips, clearly gearing up to argue. He didn't intend to give her a chance. "Honey, you driving him home amounts to throwing kibble at the dog for pissing in the corner. He wants your attention right now. Give it to him and you train him to follow his worst instincts. None of it's your fault," he added, because he remembered spending too many hours of his life wondering why he couldn't learn to stay the fuck out of Big Joe's crosshairs. "But if you want a couple of minutes to talk to him before I come out and put him in my truck, better take them right now."

To soften the words, or maybe to distract himself from the defeated look in her eyes, he traced his finger along her jaw.

"Tyler," she sighed, infusing his name with a universe of pent-up emotion.

"Ellie," he replied calmly, keeping his tone matter-of-fact, but unwavering.

She stared at him for another moment while she analyzed her options, and then turned and strode out of the bedroom without a backward glance.

He dressed fast, one ear on the conversation out front. Frank started into a rant about her telling Rawley's not to serve him. Ellie denied telling anyone not to serve him, and suggested perhaps they refused his business because they were sick of dealing with him at times like this, when he was drunk and belligerent. She told him he'd feel better if he went home, ate something, and got some sleep.

The lower and cooler Ellie's voice went, the louder and more agitated Frank became. By the time Tyler approached the door, Frank had resorted to shouting grievances. He didn't need her checking up on him and telling him what to do. She disrespected him, walked around like she was better than everyone just because she had a few letters after her name.

Tyler stepped onto the porch and let the screen door bang shut. In the copper glow of the porch light, he watched Frank's head swivel around and his squinty, bloodshot eyes try to focus.

"Time to go, Frank."

It took a minute, but awareness finally dawned across the older man's features. Then his attention bounced back to his daughter. His gaze raked over her disheveled hair, bare feet, and bathrobe. "You're not better than me," he yelled. "You're nothing but a—"

"Get in the truck," Tyler interrupted, out of patience. Frank didn't move, so Tyler gripped the man's withered bicep and walked him down the porch steps.

"Take your hands off me," Frank growled.

He tried to jerk free, but stumbled instead. Tyler quickly

had his hands full keeping them both upright, and took a fist to his jaw for his efforts. His head snapped back. He heard his teeth click together a second before he tasted blood.

"God*dam*mit," he cursed.

"Come on," Frank challenged, jaw jutting while he staggered around on the tether of Tyler's arm like a muleheaded prizefighter. "Take a shot."

Ellie rushed over and stepped between them, proving muleheadedness ran in the family. "Jesus, I'm sorry," she said, and angled his head down so she could examine his jaw.

"Stop." He turned, forcing her to his other side, using his body to block her from Frank's reach.

She stuck to him like a spider web, wincing as she eyed him. "You're bleeding."

And hoping like hell to be the only one, so for God's sake, back the hell away from the punch-throwing drunk. Instead of barking the words at her, he took a deep breath and counted to ten. Then, in a pissy-sounding voice he couldn't believe came from his own throat, he said, "Don't doctor me."

She opened her mouth to object, so he pointed a finger at her. "You, go inside. You"—he swung the finger Frank's way—"in the truck."

They both blinked at him.

"*Now.*"

That got them moving. Frank clambered up into the passenger seat of the truck. Ellie retreated to the porch. Satisfied things were going to resolve without further bloodshed, Tyler pulled his keys from the front pocket of his jeans and got behind the wheel.

"I'll be in touch," he said to Ellie, and slowly reversed out of her driveway.

Chapter Fourteen

Ellie closed the door, rested her forehead against the smooth wood, and let tears burn their way down her cheeks. There were worse catastrophes than having her father show up drunk and punch the man she was sleeping with. None sprang to mind, but realistically, she knew they existed.

A few other thoughts did spring to mind, though. Thoughts like, she didn't know how to handle Frank anymore. Their relationship remained as dysfunctional as ever, but now, with the added bonus of the diabetes and an escalating drinking problem, her old "do your duty" approach no longer worked. She needed a new one, but unfortunately, short of hiring round-the-clock caretakers—a solution he'd never accept and she couldn't afford anyway—she had no ideas.

Sniffing back tears, she trudged down the hall to her bedroom. Big mistake. The ridiculous, hot-pink vibrator lay on the bed, reminding her of the excitement, passion, and plain old *fun* she and Tyler had shared earlier in the evening. A sound somewhere between a laugh and a sob hiccuped from her throat. She pressed her fist over her chest and faced facts.

She'd be lucky if he ever spoke to her again, much less laid a hand on her. Even if he did call her, what on earth would she say? *Sorry about my dad. I promise it won't happen again?* Right. Pretty clearly she couldn't deliver on such a promise. If she had the power to make Frank behave the way she wanted, tonight never would have happened in the first place.

She crossed to the bed, tossed the vibrator into her nightstand drawer, and faced another fact. The ache in her chest stemmed not from the permanent derailment of her master plan, or from losing her tutor, but from losing *Tyler*. That loss hurt the most, which didn't even make any sense, considering their deal had been temporary by design. But somehow, whenever she spent time with him, he managed to fog her brain, sweep her off her feet, and make her lose sight of her plans.

He shouldn't have been able to do any of it. Her mind came equipped with automatic defrost to prevent dangers such as fogging. She always kept her sights on her goals, and she never, ever got swept off her feet.

A balled-up crumple of purple lace sticking out from the corner of one pillow mocked those contentions. She picked up her underwear and stuffed it in the pocket of her robe. Forget about feet, Tyler swept her right out of her panties with startling regularity.

Why do you suppose that is? a worried voice in the back of her head questioned.

Because he's been separating females from their panties since high school. He's good at it, which is why you wanted him as your tutor. Too bad tonight had undoubtedly sent him running for the hills. Thanks to her inability to handle her own father, she'd never learn how to seduce Roger. Good-bye golden-haired tykes pedaling little red bikes in front of a brick Tudor on Riverview. Good-bye Sundays in pew four.

Maybe she ought to consider tonight a wake-up call. She probably wasn't cut out to be part of a large, supportive family any more than she was cut out to be a wild woman, she thought grimly as she plopped down on her bed.

Immediately restless, she shot up again and stalked to her closet. Sitting at home talking to herself did no one any good. Driving out to check on Frank at least put her medical training to use.

Fifteen minutes later she made the turn from the old highway into the subdivision she'd called home for her first eighteen years. A black pickup truck coming from the opposite direction flashed its headlights at her.

Tyler.

She pulled over. The side of the road was as good a place as any for him to officially cancel the rest of their classes. Her heart thumped hard in her chest as he approached, creating an anxious backbeat to the crunch of his boots on the roadside.

He crouched by her window and looked at her.

She looked back, throat tightening as she inspected his abused jaw. Her fingers twitched to inspect the area, make sure he was okay. Through sheer force of will, she kept her hands on the steering wheel. Still, he must have read her thoughts, because he said, "It's fine, Ellie."

Something about his low, calm voice cracked a dam of anger inside her. She watched in shocked detachment as her hands fisted and slammed against the steering wheel. A voice she barely recognized erupted from her throat. "It is *not* fine. My father hit you. You're not fine. He's not fine. *I'm* not fine!"

He had her out of the car and wrapped in his arms in the next instant, her face pressed against his chest so she felt the sure, steady beat of his heart under her cheek. She shivered uncontrollably despite the hot summer night and the warmth of his body surrounding her. Worse, she sobbed like a deranged banshee.

Tyler just held her, patient and silent, as if they weren't standing on the roadside at midnight, and let her cry herself dry. It took a while. Finally, light-headed and raw in the throat, she raised her head back and rubbed the heels of her hands over her burning eyes.

"Oh, my God. I'm sorry." She looked at the huge soggy spot in the center of his T-shirt. Tears and sweat and God only knew what else. "I think I owe you a shirt."

"I owe you a pair of panties. We'll call it even." He tipped her chin up and inspected her face. "Feeling better?"

"Yes." *If humiliated counts as better.* She drew away from him until she stood on her own two feet. "Again, I'm sorry—"

"Don't apologize. What happened with Frank tonight? It's not your fault."

"He drinks too much."

"Not your fault."

"He's angry because…well…" She sighed. "He's always angry."

"He's angry at God, fate, the world. That's also not your fault."

The bone-deep certainty in his words made her want to cry again, so she forced her lips into a weak smile. "So what you're saying is, this is not my fault?"

Tyler smiled back. "Something like that, yeah."

She looked away. "That's nice of you to say, but father-daughter relationships probably aren't your area of expertise."

"You might be surprised to hear this, but my expertise isn't limited to sex."

His dry tone drew her attention back to his face. She didn't know what she expected to see in his expression, but it wasn't the reluctant look of someone about to discuss something he clearly preferred not to talk about. The impression strengthened when he lifted the hem of his shirt and pointed to the scar running down his side.

"You asked me once how I got this. Still wanna know?"

She nodded.

"When I was twelve, Big Joe took a swipe me with the claw end of a hand ax because I didn't stack the firewood right. He'd been drinking, because he always drank, and he'd been pissed off already, because he was always pissed off. It wasn't the first or last time he let me know in no uncertain terms he wasn't happy with me."

A vision of Joe Longfoot formed in her mind: large, intimidating, with quick, hard eyes, and a mouth twisted into a permanent sneer. Unable to stop herself, she stepped close and gently touched the scar. Tears stung her eyes, picturing Tyler at twelve, defenseless against his own father, who should have protected him, taken care of him...loved him. "That's awful," she whispered.

"Yeah." He took her hand and squeezed gently. "When your mom drops you off on the first day of kindergarten and never comes back, and your dad knocks the crap out of you every time you screw up, you start to wonder if maybe you're the problem."

Outraged that he could even think such a thing, she blurted, "Of course you weren't the problem. *They* were the problem. You were an innocent victim."

His pointed look cut her off.

She shook her head. "My situation is different."

"It's not. Not one damn bit. I wasted years trying to figure out what I'd done to deserve being abandoned by my mother and knocked around by my dad. Eventually I realized my parents' issues had nothing to do with me. My mother lit out because she couldn't take my dad's temper anymore. She sacrificed me to save herself because I think she figured if she took me and left him with nobody to knock around, he'd come after us. Maybe she was right, but right or wrong, I could have been the best kid in the world and it wouldn't have changed her decision. Same with Joe. I didn't turn him into a big, mean son of a bitch. He'd been one before I came along and he stayed one 'til the day he died."

Her rational, logical side understood his point, but some weak, emotional part of her balked at drawing a parallel between Tyler's family and her own. There were differences. Big differences. Her mother was gone. Nothing could change that. His might be alive and well, grappling with regret, hoping to reconnect with the son she'd abandoned.

"Your mom…has she, or have you ever…?" She couldn't get the rest of the question past the lump in her throat.

"No. I haven't heard from her or seen her since she left." He said the words quietly. "I've never tried to find her."

"Do you hate her?"

"Hate's the wrong word. At this point in my life, I can see her situation a little more clearly than I did as a kid. She was only twenty-three, and stuck in a love-hate relationship with a man who was probably going to be the death of her if she stayed put. So she ran. I understand why, but I can't quite forgive her. She's never looked me up, and I'm not hard to find considering I've always been pretty much right where she left me, so I figure she's not desperate to reconnect. For me"—he shrugged—"it's done. I don't really need a parent anymore."

"I do." Admitting it made her understand why she needed to claim some responsibility for the problems with Frank. If she owned part of the problem, she could own part of the solution. Otherwise, Frank controlled everything, and he might never reach out to her.

She looked up at the moon and blinked fast. "Stupid, I know." From the corner of her eye, she caught his sympathetic look and her heart twisted. "I never admitted this to anyone, but the main reason I came home to open my practice was because I thought I could fix things between Frank and me. I told myself he needed me now, because of the diabetes. I'd help him, and in doing so, prove I'm no longer an unwanted responsibility my mom left behind when she died. He'd be grateful, admire the grown-up me, and want us to be a real family—"

"He might."

"Yeah, right. He hates when I come around, tells me I'm lecturing him when I try to help."

"Yeah, but he's always there, isn't he?"

She didn't know what to say to that.

"People can change. You've shown him what's at stake by coming back. Maybe now it's time to back off and see whether he can get his act together and make the changes?"

"I should go check on him, test his glucose."

"No, you shouldn't."

"He could be—"

Tyler's unwavering stare stilled her tongue. "Frank's okay. He had a bite to eat and then we had a little heart-to-heart about his options. He needs some time alone to think things over and decide what he wants to do."

"I don't understand. His options?"

"I told him I'd keep those between us. He'll tell you if he wants you to know."

"This is..." At a loss, she thumped her tire with the sole of her flip-flop. "You expect me to just...get in my car and drive away?"

"You're going to stop by tomorrow evening anyway, right? He told me you bring groceries on Saturdays."

"Yes, but—"

"Tomorrow's soon enough. What are you doing afterward?"

"Excuse me?"

"What are you doing tomorrow night after you stop at

Frank's?"

"Um...nothing."

"Want some help doing nothing?"

• • •

She looked so stumped by his invitation he nearly laughed. "C'mon, Ellie. It's too late to tell me you have to wash your hair. How about you come by my place after you stop by Frank's?"

"You want to get together again? After everything?"

"Seems like this evening's lesson ended prematurely." As soon as he said the words, he wished them back. Yes, he wanted to see her tomorrow, but not so they could finish lesson whatever-the-hell number they were on. He should have asked her to dinner or a movie...a real date. He wasn't an expert at telling a woman "I'm falling in love with you," but he suspected the words were supposed to be accompanied by a few romantic gestures, and an orgasm probably didn't qualify. But when Ellie responded to his comment with a big, cheek-dimpling smile, he knew he'd dangled the right bait. Disappointing, but he'd use whatever worked to keep her coming back until she finally realized she wanted more from him than wild sex.

"Seven okay?" he asked.

"Seven is perfect. I'll bring dinner."

A cozy dinner at his place had "real date" potential. Could be she already thought he might be good for something besides wild sex.

"Afterward," she went on, "maybe we could—?"

"Anything you want."

"Seriously?"

"Seriously, Doc. Anything you want to do."

• • •

"You really want to do this?" Tyler asked, letting his tone convey his reluctance, which he'd already expressed straight-out, multiple times.

Ellie dropped her forehead to her forearms. "For the umpteenth time, yes." Lifting her head, she turned and stared over her shoulder. "You promised."

His dick didn't want to argue. The sight of her kneeling on all fours in front of him, naked and dewy from the rain-heralding humidity, had that particular part of him straining to comply, but his brain kept interfering. "You don't know what you want. You've never done this before."

"I know I want to try, because the book says men love chapter 13. It gets five stars, for crying out loud."

"I'll bet in the book on how to drive women wild, it gets zero stars."

"If you ever take lessons on driving women wild, you don't have to pick this. Look, nothing's wrong with my power of speech. If I don't like it, I'll tell you to stop, okay? I trust you."

He scrubbed his hand over his face. How could he argue with trust? "You win. Where's the lube?"

She grabbed it from the nightstand and passed the tube to him. "I thought you said as long as you had two hands and a tongue we wouldn't need lube?"

"I stand corrected. Now shut up."

He entertained himself for a few minutes rubbing lube over her, concentrating on familiar territory he knew she liked, basically massaging between her legs until she moaned and rocked into his touch. Sure, he was stalling, but she didn't seem to mind—

"Tyler, this is all very nice, and"—he slipped a finger inside her tight, wet channel—"oh…jeez, stimulating, but—"

Yeah, but. "All right, hold on a second." With his free hand he felt around on the bed until he found what he was looking for. Another dab of lube, and he nudged his way along the cleft between her cheeks to his target. Then he pressed very, very gently.

"That's not...so bad," she said, her voice rising at the end because she squirmed to try and hurry him along.

"That's Thumper."

She stilled. "Thumper?"

"Yep." He could almost hear the gears in her brain turning as she ran her calculations. He was bigger, wider, and longer than the vibrator. Thank God he'd told her to bring the thing tonight. He might have to rename it "The Deal Breaker."

Ellie flipped over, wrapped her arms around her drawn-up knees and stared at him with huge eyes. "You're right. I don't want to do this."

"Good." Gripping her hips, he hauled her up into his arms, one hand supporting the ass she'd been so anxious to give him a piece of, the other fanned across her back. Her hands flew to his shoulders at the same time her legs clamped around his waist. Ignoring her squeak of surprise, he stood. "I've got a better idea. Grab the blanket, will you? My hands are full."

"Oh-kay." Despite the skeptical reply, she reached down and snagged the lightweight blue quilt.

He carried her down the hall and straight out the back door. The big, glowing orb of a moon turned her skin alabaster and edged the quickly encroaching rainclouds bunched low over the treetops with silver.

"Tyler, have you lost your mind? It's going to rain."

He stopped in the flat, grassy area in the middle of his oak-shrouded yard. "You won't melt. Drop the blanket."

She did. He toed the edges out into a square, then sank to his knees and lowered her until she lay across the spread. His breath hitched at the picture she made, bathed in moonlight.

Still not the right setting to bare his soul and tell her he wanted to be more to her than...hell...the guy who'd talked her out of chapter 13, but maybe he could show her. He crawled over her. She smiled up at him and shivered.

"Cold?"

"No. This is the best I've felt all day. You're right. I won't melt."

Well, hopefully she would, but not from a little rain. He leaned in and covered her soft, smiling lips with his, sinking into a long, hot, wet, endless kiss.

"I don't remember the naked backyard campout chapter from the handbook," she said, a bit breathlessly, when he lifted his head.

"Not everything worth learning is summarized in a book. Sometimes you've got to rely on instincts." To prove his point, he cupped her jaw and kissed her again, worshipping her mouth, not stopping until she clutched his shoulders and made urgent little sounds in the back of her throat. When he looked down at her this time, dazed brown eyes stared back at him.

"I'm not sure what the lesson is, Tyler." Her whispered admission and concerned look sent flames licking hungrily up his abdomen and spreading into his chest. Type A Ellie liked to know the rules, liked knowing what to expect. Flying blind made her nervous. He prepared to make her all kinds of nervous.

"Trust me."

"I do. But..."

Her voice trailed off when he put his lips to work on her jaw, her throat, the smooth curve where neck became shoulder. "I could kiss you all night," he murmured against her skin.

"You couldn't. You'd get chapped lips," she managed, spearing her fingers in his hair and bowing her spine as he flicked his tongue over her perfect, pebbled nipple.

He laughed and transferred his attention to her other breast. "Can't help it. You're so beautiful."

The fingers in his hair stilled. "You don't have to say things like that."

"Like what?" He kissed the soft swell directly over her heart. "The truth?"

He *did* have to say things like "you're beautiful," he realized, feathering his fingertips down her fluttering stomach, because she honestly didn't know. How could he have overlooked the words for this long? Time to fix the oversight.

"You're beautiful here..." He kissed her stunned mouth.

"Tyler, don't—"

"And here." He brushed his lips over the vulnerable hollow at the base of her throat and swallowed a satisfied smile when her pulse beat an erratic rhythm under his lips.

"Don't..." she gasped again, arching involuntarily when he swirled his tongue around her belly button. It took a few beats for her to find her voice, but eventually, her weak, "I'm not," reached his ears.

"You don't have the first clue, do you?" He wedged his shoulders between her legs and kissed the point of her hip. "How beautiful you are. Every inch of you..." His voice dropped and he kissed her between her thighs, where she was already hot and wet.

Her head tipped back and strangled denial caught in her throat. He kept right on kissing her, licking, sucking, swirling his tongue over her until she shivered uncontrollably.

Moving up her body, linking his fingers with hers, he brought their joined hands to rest on either side of her head. "Look at me, Ellie."

Chapter Fifteen

Ellie hadn't realized she'd closed her eyes, but now she opened them and fell into the endless emerald depths of Tyler's. As their gazes connected, she sensed his delivered a message. Insight flickered at the edge of her consciousness like a candle burning at midnight, but then he drove into her, flooding her overloaded system with sensations, extinguishing thought.

She barely felt the first drops of cool summer rain strike her feverish skin.

He set the pace, slow and thorough, and stoked the hungry need building and centering inside her with each incredible thrust. Warmth escalated to heat. Heat turned to fire, and still he watched. The rain caressing her skin only fed the flames. His breath against her cheek only fanned the blaze.

Control ran through her hands like water. Not good. This wasn't what she'd bargained for. She flexed her fingers and tested the careful but unbreakable prison of his grip. She must have made a frustrated noise when she couldn't pull free, because he whispered, "Don't. If you touch me, this will be over in three seconds. Just let me have you."

"Not like this, it's too—" Too intimate? Too intense? She couldn't put the fear into words, but suddenly, the thought of staring into his all-seeing eyes while she shattered in his arms terrified her, even as every cell in her body ached to do just that.

"Before, in the bedroom, you said you trusted me. Trust me now and let go. I want to watch your eyes go dark and dreamy, I want to hear that little cry you make right before you come. I want to feel your body tremble for me."

The words alone made her tremble. What he didn't seem to appreciate was that she had no choice—he had her completely at his mercy and every long, leisurely stroke sharpened her need to a critical, almost painful point. Or maybe he knew and simply didn't care, but no amount of writhing on her part altered his slow, measured thrusts. Her breath came in erratic pants, and still he tortured her with the sweet, unhurried rhythm. Stroking, stroking...always stroking, until she couldn't concentrate on anything except the slick, hot slide of him over her swollen, aching flesh.

"Let go," he repeated, thrusting harder, reaching deeper.

She couldn't stifle a helpless moan of pleasure, but endured another flash of insight— this one as profound and powerful as his body buried in hers. *Let go?* She'd let go a while back, without even realizing it. Maybe weeks ago, when he'd shrugged off her carefully prepared lesson and taken her out on his motorcycle instead, or days ago, when he'd gone all the way to Lexington to shop for something as ridiculous as sex toys, or last night, when he'd held her in his arms at the side of the road and let her cry all over him. Somewhere along the line she'd handed this man way more than her body. While she struggled against that revelation, Tyler whispered, "Now," gathered her close, and drove into her with one final, devastating thrust.

She let go. He held on. They both went flying.

"I love you," tumbled from her lips.

• • •

Despite Tyler's big, heavy, incredibly warm body covering hers, Ellie shivered as she stared at the stars peeking through wispy clouds. The storm had passed, but now the rapid beat of her heart replaced the cadence of falling rain.

Had she actually spewed the words "I love you," or had she imagined it? Either answer scared her senseless. Tyler and she were completely wrong for each other. She yearned for the ties and connections of a big, tight-knit family, a sense of belonging. Things she'd never experienced. Neither had Tyler, but unlike her, he'd spent his entire adult life avoiding them. Even if he suddenly decided to trade late nights at Rawley's and a revolving-door love life for commitments and responsibilities, how could they possibly succeed? Talk about the blind leading the blind. What did either of them know firsthand about happy homes? Absolutely nothing.

Home and family defined Roger as intrinsically as his blue eyes and ready smile. His loving, supportive upbringing counterbalanced everything hers lacked. Filial bonds, a sense of purpose and destiny based simply on being a Reynolds, were practically woven into his DNA. And he'd be on her doorstep Monday night, ready to meet a sexually experienced, confident woman, not some confused girl who'd accidentally fallen for the wrong man. She'd had a plan. How had her heart gone so completely off course?

A groan sneaked past her lips before she could bite it back. Tyler immediately shifted and mumbled, "Sorry. I'm crushing you." Head propped in his hand, he looked down at her, his expression unreadable.

"No, no. It's not you. I'm just, um..." Her flight instinct

kicked in. "I've got to go." She said the words quickly because her stupid heart wanted to stay right where she was, at his side, forever.

"Something spook you, Doc?"

Was he toying with her? She sat up and scooted away from him before her hands gave in to the temptation of his broad shoulders and the carved muscles of his chest. "No, of course not."

He edged closer. She inched back.

"You seem a little jumpy. Let's talk."

"Talk?" God, she sounded like a parrot.

"Yeah. I'll start. A few minutes ago, you told me, 'I—'"

"I have to go!" Her mind shuffled for a plausible exit strategy. "I need to check on Frank. He wasn't home when I dropped off groceries after work."

Tyler's eyes narrowed. "Frank is MIA?"

"No," she admitted, hating the quiver in her voice. "He left a note saying he was at a meeting."

"So what's to check? He was at a meeting." His raised eyebrow implied her excuse fell short of convincing.

She scrambled to her feet and shook her head. "Frank doesn't have meetings. He has Rawley's—when they serve him—and his couch. His note doesn't make any sense. Nothing makes any sense." Least of all her. She took a step back, then another. "Good luck with the bank on Tuesday. I'll see you...around."

• • •

Tyler stared up at the big ghost-white moon. The craggy face seemed to laugh at him, and he supposed the whole thing did play like some kind of joke. He, the king of the loose, casual hookup, just produced an "I love you" from the only woman who mattered, and she ran off so fast she practically left a vapor trail in her wake.

Still, it was hard to appreciate the humor of the situation with his heart bleeding out of his chest. He'd intended to say the words, eventually, but in the proper setting, with the right lead-in. Say the words first and be prepared to deal with her doubts. He knew damn well she had them. Doubts about the chances of two people like them, who'd never known love, creating one that lasted a lifetime.

He hadn't said the words, even though he felt them. She had, and it should have thrilled him, but it sucked. Not only because she hadn't meant to say it, but because afterward, she'd looked at him like some kind of dead-end detour she'd accidentally taken. She'd certainly thrown herself into reverse and hauled ass in the other direction as quickly as she could. Somewhere deep inside, a part of him insisted her reaction affirmed a lesson he should have learned when his mother left. Namely, he wasn't the kind of guy women stuck around for, invested in, or planned on spending forever with.

Another part of him recognized the thoughts as Big Joe talking in his head, telling him he wasn't good enough. He'd done his best to ignore his father when alive. He sure as hell shouldn't listen to a dead man.

He should listen to his gut. And his gut told him Ellie loved him. The knowledge rattled her. Understandable, considering how much she liked her plans. She felt safe with everything mapped out, and loving him threw her into uncharted territory. She'd need a moment to get her bearings, sort out her feelings. Maybe more than a moment, but the point was, she needed time.

He'd give her 'til Monday. Then ready or not, they were going to talk.

Chapter Sixteen

Ellie stared into her bedroom mirror and adjusted the strapless top of the short, red scarf of a dress she'd chosen as her drive-Roger-wild outfit—just one more detail of her meticulously orchestrated evening. During the past forty-eight hours she'd reaffirmed her ability to push distractions aside, stay the course, and stick to a damn plan. Of course, it helped that she'd had a zillion things to accomplish in preparation for tonight.

No time for worries about where Frank had been Saturday evening when she'd stopped by, or hours later when she'd driven past his darkened house on her way home from Tyler's. She'd shoved those concerns to the back burner and strategized every nuance of her date with Roger, from the menu, to her outfit, to, most importantly, which chapters she'd employ to prove she was his ideal woman.

Whenever her irrational internal debate about what, if anything, Tyler had thought of her heat-of-passion outburst Saturday night threatened to interrupt her efforts, she'd ruthlessly silenced those voices. The questions had absolutely no bearing on tonight. He didn't belong in her head. Right now she needed to give her entire focus to her Win Roger Plan, because tonight's date represented a critical milestone.

She touched up her makeup and ticked through her mental checklist for the evening. Seductive hair? Check. The tousled updo artfully suggested she'd just gotten out of bed and could be talked back in with very little effort. Enticing outfit? Check. The wispy little dress looked like a stiff breeze could blow it off. The super-high red heels she'd bought to go with it screamed "Screw me. *Now*." Basically, she'd never worn a sexier ensemble in her life.

Too bad she'd never felt less sexy, or more nauseous. Nerves or...something...had sunk a cold ball of dread in the pit of her stomach. The ball rolled uneasily every time she thought about Roger here, in her bedroom, or the two of them delving into any of the chapters she'd mastered. Performance anxiety? Maybe. She blotted the sweat on her forehead and told herself to calm down.

Then the doorbell chimed and calm officially left the building. She forced her lips into a smile and hurried to the door.

Roger stood there, pale under his golden tan, hands smoothing his white linen shirt over his khaki pants.

"Hello, Roger. Please come in." God, she sounded like an undertaker.

"Thanks. Oh, my goodness." He blushed to the roots of his hair. "You look so...gosh, what's the word?"

For some reason, his stammering reaction only ratcheted up her tension. She felt like she was sitting on a roller coaster perched at the top of the very first drop, and suddenly realized she didn't want to take the plunge. All this time she'd been following her plan, so bent on achieving her goal that she'd ignored every click of conscience warning her she was going farther and farther along the wrong track. The Roger she wanted was a fantasy of her own creation, not a real man. In reality she barely knew the man standing on her doorstep, and she certainly wasn't in love with him.

"Ellie, I think maybe you've got the wrong—"

"Roger, I'm so sorry, but I can't—"

Their words overlapped and they both stopped short, leaving a deafening silence. Roger broke it with a weak laugh. "Sorry. Ladies first."

"No, I'm the sorry one." She sighed and let out a long breath. "I know you're expecting wild, Slap & Tickle-style sex tonight—and I wanted you to think that's exactly the kind of woman I am—but I'm not and, I'm sorry, I just can't. I'm an idiot for dragging you out here under false pretenses."

She glanced at him from beneath her lashes, surprised to see his jaw relax and a faint smile tug at his lips. "I think when it comes to false pretenses, I win the prize."

"I don't understand."

"No, but you deserve to. Can we sit down and talk?"

So much for hostess of the year. "Of course," she said quickly, and led him into the front room, turning on lights as she went and blowing out the ridiculous candles she'd placed everywhere. They sat on the sofa, facing each other. If he noticed the soft, sax-heavy music oozing from the sound system or the iced bottle of champagne and duo of flutes on the end table, he didn't comment. Instead he took her hand in his and stared into her eyes. "I didn't ask to see you tonight because I expected for us to have sex. I'm…" He exhaled and looked away. "This is harder than I imagined."

She put a hand on his arm. "You can tell me anything."

His eyes met hers again. "I'm gay."

Gay? Roger was gay? Her mind went blank, and then replayed a montage of scenes that took on new and completely obvious meaning. She remembered how wistfully he'd spoken about his friend from New York the evening she'd removed his splinter, and how uncomfortable he'd been introducing Doug at Slap & Tickle. Lord, she'd been so blind.

"You and Doug?"

He nodded. "Yes. I'm sorry. I thought you figured it out the night you saw us together at Slap & Tickle. Doug said no, but I was paranoid. We both realized Tyler knew, and I figured he'd out me, though I shouldn't have. He's not that kind of person. When you and I spoke the next morning at Jiffy Java, your responses made me think you knew. That's why I asked if we could get together and talk. I wanted to explain—to tell you I'm trying really hard to keep my orientation private. Hardly anyone here knows."

"But...Melody?"

Roger offered a pained smile. "Yes, she knows. Knew before I did, actually. She asked me a couple years ago if maybe I was gay. I didn't want to be, and I didn't want to let her go, so I told her no. But when I moved home earlier this year, I couldn't hide from the truth anymore. I missed Doug so much, even though we never...I mean, I was engaged to Melody and I always honored our commitment, in body if not in heart. She saw my misery, though, and for obvious reasons our relationship wasn't exactly her dream come true either. So I finally opened up to her about everything. We talked, cried, promised we'd always be friends, and then we called off our engagement."

His eyes glistened as he talked, and Ellie got an instant picture of how painful the last few months had been for him. And Melody. God, she owed Melody a huge apology for misunderstanding her reaction. All she'd been trying to do was prevent Ellie from embarrassing herself.

This is what you get for eavesdropping, her conscience chimed in, reminding her why she'd hatched the whole insane plan in the first place. "When I got back into town, one of the first things I heard, well, overheard technically, was that you two broke up because you wanted a high-adventure sex life and Melody didn't."

"Yeah, the story was Mel's idea. We both knew the news of our broken engagement would cause a rustle in the local grapevine. After a ten-year engagement, an explanation like 'It just didn't work out' doesn't quite satisfy people. She thought spreading the rumor about my wild, insatiable sexual appetites would distract the rumor mill and help me keep the real reason under wraps. I'm truly sorry, Ellie. I never dreamed you had any romantic interest in me, or I would have been honest with you right away."

"Don't apologize. I had the truth staring me in the face and chose not to see it because I was too busy chasing a fairy tale."

"Now I don't understand."

"It's hard to explain, even to myself, but I created an idealized image of you in my mind, based strictly on my needs, and I wouldn't let little things like reality intrude. I thought if you and I fell in love, we'd live happily ever after and...poof... all the frustrations and disappointments in my life would magically disappear. You come from such a perfect, loving family, and I wanted to be part of one so badly, I put together an elaborate scheme to win you. I tried to change myself into your fantasy woman."

"Sweetie." He rubbed her arm. "My family isn't perfect. We're no prize. One of the reasons I'm paranoid about news of my being gay leaking is because I'm pretty sure Dad would have a coronary. Mom would go straight to Bluelick Baptist and pray. I'm too much of a coward to tell them the truth, but I'm too selfish to stay here pretending to be something I'm not. Instead, I'll disappoint them by moving back to New York, and they'll never understand why. They'll think I rejected their love and everything they worked so hard to give me, when in reality, I don't deserve it."

She took his hands and waited until his tortured eyes locked on hers. "You deserve the things they want to give you, including their love. You're a good son, a talented lawyer, and a compassionate person. But you're also an adult, entitled to lead your own life. Lead it honestly and proudly. Tell your folks. Their reaction might surprise you. But more importantly, you'll respect yourself."

He blinked hard and swallowed. "You sound just like Melody."

"Melody's awfully smart." Ellie squeezed his arm and then rose.

Roger rose as well and followed her to the front door. He paused at the threshold. "There's something I'm curious about."

"What's that?"

"You thought Melody and I broke up because I wanted, as you put it, a high-adventure sex life, and you decided to turn yourself into the kind of woman who could deliver high adventure. I'm wondering exactly how you went about that?"

She winced. "Believe me, it wasn't easy. I had a *lot* to learn." Tyler's sexy grin popped into her head.

"Was visiting Slap & Tickle with Tyler part of the learning curve, by any chance?"

Heat swept into her cheeks. "Yes. Poor Tyler. I made him give me lessons on how to drive a man wild."

Roger's eyes widened and then he fanned his face. "When you come up with a plan, you don't mess around, do you? Go straight to the hottest guy in town and say, 'Show me the ropes!'"

He looked so astounded and impressed she had to laugh. "Yeah, I'm a real class act."

"Class-schmass. If I was single and could think of a way to convince Tyler to show *me* the ropes, I'd do it in a heartbeat. But, unfortunately, he's not into me, so he'd find a charming way to turn me down, because under the cocky exterior, he's a decent, fundamentally good guy."

He was all of those things and much more. She couldn't deny the truth anymore…she loved him. But Saturday night, when her feelings had bubbled to the surface, she'd run away like a scared little girl, hell-bent on chasing her fairy tale instead of taking a real-life risk on happily ever after.

"Interestingly," Roger went on, "he didn't turn *you* down, so I'm guessing he is into you."

"I don't know." Making guesses about Tyler's motives caused a flood of guilt and anxiety. She prayed his offer to talk still stood.

Roger grinned, a little mischievously. "He showed you the ropes, didn't he?"

She couldn't suppress a smile. "He sure did."

"Now you're just bragging, so I'm going to take off. Thanks for being so understanding. I hope we're still friends."

"Absolutely." Framed by the doorway, she rose onto her tiptoes and hugged him. He hugged back, wrapping his big arms around her and pulling her close.

"Give me one of those 'show me the ropes' kisses, Sparky," he whispered. "It's the closest I'll ever come to kissing Tyler."

Laughing, she cupped Roger's cheeks, stared into his magnificent blue eyes, and planted a big, fat kiss on his lips. *Good-bye, handsome prince.* He swept her into a dramatic dip. She squealed and held onto him.

He raised his head and he winked at her. "Wow. You're one lucky woman. And something tells me if he plays his cards right, Tyler's one lucky guy."

An engine revved, interrupting her reply. Even from her upside-down vantage point in Roger's arms, she could make out the blur of a motorcycle racing away.

"Oh, shit." Roger slowly straightened. "Mr. Lucky just raced off into the night. I think maybe he got the wrong idea.

Want me to go after him and explain?"

Shit. Shit. Shit! She tamped down the panic threatening to choke her and shook her head. "No, I need to talk to him about…a lot of things. This is mine to fix."

"Okay." He touched her cheek lightly and then stepped away. "Let me know how things turn out. I'm rooting for you."

"Same goes. I'm rooting for you, too, no matter what you decide to do."

He smiled and headed out into the warm summer night. Inside the house, Beethoven's Fifth sounded. With a final wave, she went in and answered the phone.

She didn't usually get calls in the evening except from her service. The display, however, read "Unknown Number." As soon as she picked up, a hesitant female voice said, "Dr. Swann?"

"Yes, this is she."

"Hello, Dr. Swann. My name is Sharon Greene. I'm a friend of your father's. I'm sorry to ambush you this way, but I need to let you know Lexington Memorial Hospital admitted him this evening after he became ill at our meeting."

"Oh, God. Is he okay? What's the diagnosis?" She cursed herself for not calling him yesterday. He probably wouldn't have picked up, but still, she should have tried.

"I don't know, Dr. Swann. He gave me your name and number before the paramedics took him away, and asked me to call you. Can you come?"

"I'm on my way."

Chapter Seventeen

"Don't try to figure women out, Ty," Junior advised. "Not even your cute little doc. You'll just end up with a migraine. Might as well ask me to kick you in the head. At least then you'd know why your head hurt." Satisfied with this gem of wisdom, Junior tossed back the rest of his beer and then placed the empty bottle on the bar and signaled Earl for another.

Tyler rubbed a hand across his face. He already felt like he'd been kicked in the head. Had felt that way since the moment he'd seen Ellie and Roger in a lip-lock on her front porch. The image still burned in his mind; her, nearly naked and completely irresistible in a scrap of a red dress, and big, blond, muscle-bound Roger not resisting her.

"She's not *my* cute little doc. I swung by her place this evening to see if she wanted to take a ride. I thought we'd go somewhere romantic and talk, but when I pulled up Roger was there and they were kissing like he'd just gotten home from war." Jesus, he sounded like a hysterical schoolgirl. He picked up his beer and took a long drink.

"Roger Reynolds?" Junior's eyebrows shot up. "Man, he gets around. I kinda thought he didn't close the deal with Melody because he batted for the other team."

"Me too, but apparently he switch-hits."

"Now that's just greedy."

"I agree. Know what really pisses me off? He leaves town for ten years, comes back and ditches Melody first thing, and everybody looks at him like some fucking do-no-wrong golden boy. I live here my entire life, spend the better chunk of it trying to run a decent business, do some good where I can, and, sure, have a little fun here and there, and everybody sees me as an irresponsible troublemaker only out for a good time."

Junior turned to look at him square on. "That's not true, Ty."

"Sure it is. Ask anybody."

Earl Rawley stopped in front of them to deliver a fresh beer to Junior. "Hey Earl," Junior said. "You think of Tyler as an irresponsible troublemaker?"

Earl frowned and sized him up. "Wouldn't say so, no. Mighta said different when he was younger, but not since he's been old enough to set foot in my establishment. He pays his tab in full, tips like a gentleman, holds his liquor fine. Never starts any trouble"—Earl aimed a hard look at Junior, and then shifted his attention back to Tyler—"but he's quick to step in when stepping-in is called for. I wish I could say the same about all my regulars." Earl punctuated his statement with another pointed look at Junior before snagging the empty bottle and walking off to serve another customer.

"See? Earl doesn't think you're an irresponsible troublemaker."

"Earl likes me 'cause I settle my bill and don't break up the place. Not exactly a ringing character endorsement."

"Okay, fine. We'll ask someone else. Hey, Red—"

"Christ, cut it out," Tyler said quickly when Junior called out to Ginny, but Junior ignored him.

"C'mere, girl. I gotta question for you."

Ginny slunk over, sleek as missile in a skintight red tank dress. Tyler immediately thought of Ellie plastered against Roger in her flirty red dress and gritted his teeth.

"Yes, boys?"

"It true you ladies think of Tyler here as only good for a one thing?"

Ginny stared at Tyler speculatively. "Well, Junior, I'm not speaking from firsthand experience, you understand, but I can confirm Ty's rep as a first-class personal toy. They don't call him Footlong Longfoot for nothing."

"Awesome," Tyler murmured. "Thanks." He pushed his beer away and started to get up from the bar.

Ginny stopped him. "Shush up, I'm not done yet. Plenty of girls around here would love to tempt big, bad Tyler Longfoot into something more than a fast thrill, but for the longest time it was pretty obvious that's all *you* wanted. Nobody minded. God knows you had some fun coming to you after growing up with Big Joe for a daddy."

"Wow, I feel much better now, knowing women have been sleeping with me because they felt sorry for me."

"Oh, please. Nobody slept with you out of pity. I'm just saying all the girls who climbed on your bike knew exactly what kind of ride to expect and decided to sit back and enjoy the scenery. You're sexy as hell and could charm the pants off my eighty-year-old auntie, but you were always up-front about what you had in mind. You never made promises you didn't intend to keep, and you never left any hard feelings behind when you eased out the door. But, alas"—she fluttered her eyelashes and sighed—"I fear those freewheeling days are over. More's the shame 'cause I never got a ride."

"Don't give up so easy, Red," Junior piped in before Tyler

could give him the shut-the-fuck-up stare. "My boy's still on the lookout for fast thrills."

Ginny shook her head at Junior, and then gave Tyler a disconcerting look. "Men are so clueless sometimes. The only thrills this one's interested in nowadays involve a certain diminutive doctor. See?" She swept Tyler's hair off his forehead in an affectionate gesture he found oddly moving. "He's got the shell-shocked eyes. We all knew it would happen one of these days, but still. If you listen closely, you can hear hearts breaking all across the county, because deep down, Tyler's always been a keeper."

"Thank you," he said softly, truly overwhelmed.

She patted his cheek. "That, or because this idiot here shot your dick off."

Beer sprayed from Junior's nose as she walked away. "Jesus." His eyes did a quick, nervous slide to Tyler's. "Nobody in their right mind thinks I shot your dick off. You want me to spread the word your nickname still fits, I will. No problem."

"Uh, no thanks. The less time people spend discussing my dick, the better."

"Well, I can't speak for anybody else around here, but to me, you've never been irresponsible or useless. You're loyal. You stick by your friends and don't hold a grudge, even when one does something crazy and stupid in a drunk, jealous fit. If Ellie can't see your good qualities, you have to find a way to make her look harder."

Tyler stared at his boots. Junior tended to look at his friends with kind eyes, but he was right about something. Tyler had been a lot of things in his life, but never a quitter. He wasn't about to become one now, with Ellie.

• • •

"He should buy a lottery ticket," the young, somewhat intense ER doctor told Ellie, "because luck was definitely on your father's side tonight. Somebody called 9-1-1 right away, based on his lethargy, confusion and his complaints about fatigue and thirst. On top of poor diet and lack of attention to his blood sugar levels, he picked up a flu, and the combination brought on ketoacidosis. Thankfully, he's responded to treatment. But if he doesn't learn to manage his diabetes better, his luck's going to run out, and one of these days he'll end up in a coma."

The hospital's harsh white corridors, sharp, astringent smell, and pervasive atmosphere of controlled chaos usually didn't rattle Ellie, but tonight the combination produced slippery waves of nausea. She concentrated on the doctor's tired, gray eyes. "I know, Dr. Pendleton. We're working on it."

His eyes flashed with something close to sympathy. "I'm sure you're doing all you can, Dr. Swann. *He* needs to work a little harder. I'm going to check on him one last time before I head home, and I'll tell him the same things I just told you. After I'm done, you're welcome to visit with him."

"Thank you. I really appreciate..." What? Saving my dad's life, caring enough to deliver a lecture to him when he's ignored all mine? "I appreciate everything."

His smile conveyed understanding. "No problem." He started to turn away, then stopped and glanced back at her. "Oh, and his friend, Ms. Greene, is in the waiting room at the end of the hall. As she isn't a spouse or relative, I wasn't able to disclose much about your father's condition. I'm sure she'd appreciate any details you'd care to share with her."

Ellie hoped her face didn't reflect her complete and utter surprise. Since when did her father have a friend decent enough to sit in a hospital waiting to hear his condition? She nodded and made her way to the waiting area, glad she'd taken three minutes to change out of the slutty red dress and into jeans and a T-shirt before she'd rushed to the hospital. In the waiting room she spotted an attractive auburn-haired woman who might have been anywhere between forty and fifty holding a Styrofoam cup and staring off into space.

"Ms. Greene?"

The woman turned. A weak smile touched her lips and she held out a pretty, manicured hand. "Yes. And you must be Dr. Swann. I'm sorry to meet you like this."

"No, no. I appreciate your calling me." She shook the woman's hand. "Can you tell me what happened to my father tonight?"

"Of course."

They settled into two of the institutional-grade black vinyl and steel interlocking chairs populating the waiting area. "Frank was exhausted, dying of thirst, and he seemed confused by simple questions. We were worried, so we called the paramedics. He handed me your card and asked me to call you right before they loaded him into the ambulance. Then they were gone, and I haven't heard anything concrete about his condition." Sharon shook her head. "Does he have—?"

"Yes, he's diabetic," Ellie supplied. "But the doctors have his blood pH stabilized. They'll monitor him while he's here, which will most likely be a few days." She swallowed a rude remark about Frank's bullheadedness before adding, "When he's on his own again, he's going to have to do a lot better at self-regulating." Because she couldn't hold back the suspicion, she went on. "Tell me, Ms. Greene, had he been drinking when this happened?"

"Call me Sharon, please. And no. Well, at first I thought maybe he'd been drinking. He had a hard time following our discussion and his breath smelled fruity, like a rum-punch, but I know he's a beer man, so that didn't really make sense. In retrospect, I'm certain he was completely sober, Dr. Swann."

"Ellie," she corrected. "'Completely sober' isn't the way people usually describe my father." She tried, but didn't succeed in keeping the bitter edge out of her voice.

Sharon patted her hand. "He's trying to change." She sounded so reassuring and hopeful. Two more qualities Frank didn't usually bring out in people. All in all, the woman seemed entirely too sweet and classy to have anything in common with her father. She also had a diamond-encrusted wedding ring on her left ring finger. "How did you say you knew Frank?"

"I didn't say. I should probably let him explain—"

Just then Ellie caught Dr. Pendleton's wave as he passed the nurses' station on his way out. "I'll go tell him he has a visitor."

The older woman's gratitude shone in her smile. "Thank you. Only if he's feeling up to it."

Ellie rose. "No problem. I'll be back soon."

Her hand shook when she reached for the door. A burning pressure swelled in her chest. Relief took many forms, she knew, including anger, but hers wouldn't do either of them any good. Tamping down on it, she steeled herself and entered the room. Her father lay in the hospital bed, eyes closed, complexion ash gray. An IV dripped into his arm. Monitors hummed and recorded details of his heart rate, oxygen levels, and blood sugars. She stepped to the foot of his bed and checked his chart. When she glanced back at him, his eyes were open and locked on her.

"How do you feel?" Safe ground. He was, after all, in a hospital.

"Thirsty."

She poured him a cup of water from the pitcher a nurse had left on the bedside cart and handed it to him.

While he drank, she moved on to the next obvious topic. "Your friend Sharon called me." She didn't know what else to say. *I told you this would happen if you didn't take care of yourself?* She had, a thousand times, but Dr. Pendleton had already covered the diabetes lecture, so what was the point? "She's in the waiting area, if you feel up to a visitor."

"In a minute. I have something to say to you first." He struggled to raise himself into a sitting position. She took the bed control from its coil around the bed rail and hit the button to elevate his head.

"That's good," he said when they were more eye-to-eye.

"What's on your mind, Frank?" This would be short visit if he started in on her about anything. Right now she should be tracking Tyler down, explaining her whole stupid plan with Roger and begging his forgiveness. Oh, yes, and praying he wasn't so mad or disgusted he'd tell her to get the hell out of his life.

"I guess I owe you an apology."

She blinked. Frank, apologizing? "For what?"

"Friday night." His eyes shifted to some point over her shoulder. "Tyler tells me I showed up at your place half-cocked, pounding on stuff and screaming at the top of my lungs. I don't remember too well."

"One of the things you pounded on was Tyler's jaw, so I suggest you save your apology for him."

"I already did. Look"—his glance bounced back to her face—"I know apologizing for the other night only touches the top of a whole big pile of crap I need to answer for where you're concerned, but I have to start somewhere."

Maybe her ears weren't working right. Or her brain. "Start what?"

"Making amends."

Who are you and what have you done with my father? she wanted to ask, but the words wouldn't come. "Why?" she managed.

"The program I joined. Apologizing and making amends

is step nine, so I'm not exactly there yet. But I figure you're here now and my stunt Friday might still be on your mind."

Her heart started beating a little faster. "Frank, what program did you join?"

"You met Sharon, right?"

"Yes."

"She's my sponsor—my Alcoholics Anonymous sponsor. If I'm going to deal with the diabetes, I need to sober up. Didn't help much today, but generally speaking."

"No, no. Generally speaking, you're absolutely right." She ran a hand through her hair and waited for the tightness in her throat to subside. "Quitting drinking is a really, really good idea." One she'd suggested many times and he'd waved off just as often.

"When Longfoot drove me home, he told me I could either get myself under control, or he'd convince you to be done with me. He also warned me that the next time I showed up anywhere cursing and throwing punches, he'd take another fist to the jaw, and then he'd press charges and have my sorry ass thrown in jail."

Ellie shook her head, battling disbelief. "Tyler told you this?"

Frank nodded. "Get sober and get my head together or he'd have me arrested and I'd never see you again. Said those were my 'options.' I've seen some good bluffs in my day, but looking at him, I knew he meant every word. I went to my first meeting Saturday night, got matched up with Sharon as my sponsor. I've been sober for"—he squinted at the clock on the wall opposite the bed—"damn near three days."

"That's amazing," she said, meaning it, even though the information about Tyler left her almost as stunned as her father's sobriety. Nobody had ever interceded in her relationship with Frank. Not even when she was little. Of course, she'd never asked for help, either. Asking for help meant letting someone know the sorry state of her home life, and the only thing more humiliating than the relationship itself would have been letting someone else know. But Tyler had seen, and he'd stepped in. Part of her wanted to be angry at his interference, but she couldn't. Not when, thanks to him, Frank was making an effort to take responsibility for his health. She owed him her gratitude, on top of everything else.

"You were at your first meeting Saturday night when I stopped by to drop off groceries?"

"Yeah. I left you a note."

"I saw. Sunday night I drove by your place around nine, but all the lights were off."

"Another meeting, and afterward, Sharon and I went and got coffee. Talked some more. She told me her story, how she lost her husband ten years back and hit the bottle hard for a long while afterward. She's been sober for five years now, but she remembers what it was like, being where I am."

"Sound like you two talked quite a bit."

"Talking is a big part of this program. I swear I never flapped my gums so much in my life as I have these past few days."

"I'll bet," she said, biting back a smile at the image of her stubborn, taciturn father sitting in a circle of sympathetic listeners, discussing his feelings. But it was exactly what he needed to do, and the knowledge that he'd taken these first shaky steps down the path to wellness left her cautiously optimistic. "Sharon's waiting to see you, if you're ready for more talking?"

"Yeah, yeah, in a minute. I, uh…you've been seeing a lot of Longfoot?"

Oh, God, they were *not* having this conversation. "Frank—"

"I just wanna say he cares about you. I hope I didn't screw anything up for you there."

She stared at the floor and blinked hard, because hot tears suddenly threatened. "No. I screwed it up all on my own."

"You've given out a lot of second chances, kid. Take one yourself."

Chapter Eighteen

"Jackets suck. Ties suck. This whole outfit sucks. I don't know how I let you talk me into this. I look like a moron and I probably sounded like one, too," Junior whispered to Tyler, as if his voice might carry down the carpeted hallway and through the closed door of the conference room at Bluelick Savings and Loan where the lending committee currently convened. Tyler folded his arms across his chest—mostly to keep from fidgeting with his own tie—and gave Junior what he hoped was a reassuring look.

"You did fine, answered all their questions cogently—"

"Ty, I don't even know what that means."

Tyler bit back a smile. "It means you sounded like you knew what you were talking about. We both did. If they don't approve the loan, it's not because we had our heads up our asses."

Grady Landry stepped out of the conference room, glanced down the hall at them, glanced away, then drew himself up and walked toward them. Tyler braced for bad news. When Grady drew even, his tombstone of a face split into a grin. He slapped Junior on the shoulder and pumped Tyler's hand. "Congratulations, boys, you got yourselves a loan."

Junior yee-hawed and returned Grady's slap, whacking the big man's shoulder hard enough to make Tyler wince, then whacking Tyler's for good measure. "Shit, Grady. I thought you were coming down here to chase us off."

Grady's smile widened. "I'm entitled to a little fun now and then." He ushered them to the lobby. "You gave the committee a solid presentation, impressed them with the project plan, the stability and skill of your team, and the numbers. Basically, you took away their reasons to say no. Go celebrate. Tyler, I'll call you when the docs are ready."

After another round of handshakes Tyler followed Junior out the door and into the midday sun. Junior punched his shoulder again. "Still think everyone sees you as an irresponsible troublemaker who's only good for one thing?"

"Maybe not the irresponsible troublemaker part, but unfortunately, the person who matters most still sees me as only good for one thing."

"You're just going to have to show her she's wrong. Get on over there and tell her Bluelick Savings and Loan decided to take a chance on you, and she should, too. Oh, and tell her I hope Frank's feeling better."

"I just saw Frank Friday night. He's fine."

Junior shot him a funny look, and then shook his head. "Okay, bad news. Ellie may, in fact, think you're only good for one thing. She hauled herself over to Lexington Memorial last night because paramedics brought Frank to the ER with some kind of complication from his diabetes. I found out this morning from Lou Ann, whose cousin works the admissions desk and was on duty when they brought him in. By the time she clocked out they listed him in good condition, but last she heard they were keeping him a few days."

Tyler stared at Junior for a minute, trying to wrap his head around the fact that Ellie hadn't called to tell him her father was in the hospital. Not for support, a ride, a shoulder to cry on—nothing.

"Hey Tyler, hold up," a voice called from behind him. He turned to see Roger crossing the street.

Fucking perfect, Tyler thought and felt sweat roll down his spine.

Junior squirmed out of his jacket, yanked his tie loose and wiped a forearm across his forehead. "Whew, I could use a sweet tea. I'm gonna run on over to Jiffy Java and get me one. You want one?"

"Yeah," Tyler managed. "I'll be right over."

Junior jogged across the square while Roger closed in.

"Hi, Tyler. I was hoping to run into you. Got a minute?"

He made a show of looking at his watch. "About a minute."

The blond man offered him a smile—one Tyler dearly wanted to knock off his face.

"Did Ellie explain what you saw last night?"

Tyler started walking to avoid giving in to a troublemaking impulse right in front of the bank. "I haven't spoken to her, but what I saw last night doesn't need any explanation."

Roger fell into step beside him. "Well, shoot. Yes it does." He clamped a hand on Tyler's arm. "Wait up."

His temper spiked. "Trust me Roger, you want to move that hand. I'm not in a 'Congratulations, the best man won' kind of mood right now."

Roger lifted his hand and held it up. "Fine. Not a problem, 'cause I didn't. Win, I mean." He ran his hand through his hair and puffed out a breath. "I'm saying this wrong. Look, Tyler, Ellie and I are friends."

"You looked real friendly last night." He tightened his jaw to bite off the rest of his words. She was free to pick her *friends*. He hadn't made her any promises beyond five playdates and hadn't asked any from her. It was on him to change that.

"Last night you caught a moment of silliness, not passion. I'd just told her..." Roger broke off and glanced around, then lowered his voice. "I'd just told Ellie I'm gay."

Okay, so the words confirmed his suspicion, but they didn't erase the lip-lock. "And she reacted by trying to show you what you were missing?"

Roger laughed. "Sort of, but not the way you think. Believe me, Tyler, what you saw wasn't her attempting to change my mind. It was more a good-bye and good-luck kind of thing."

Tyler took a deep breath and released it slowly. "So, you and Ellie aren't—?"

"Nope," Roger said, shaking his head.

"And she's not attracted to you?"

"Thanks for rubbing it in, but no, she's not. She'd talked herself into believing she ought to want me, but she doesn't. And she reached that conclusion before I told her the truth about myself. I could be the straightest guy in town and it wouldn't change the way she feels. I'm not the one for her. If you want my opinion, I'd say her heart is already spoken for, but she's afraid to trust what it's telling her." He smiled and backed up a step. "I think if someone grew a pair of balls to replace the set Junior shot off, and told her how *he* felt—"

"You know, I'm getting tired of folks around here speculating about my equipment."

Roger grinned and took another step away. "Maybe you ought to make a bold move and prove us all wrong."

"Yeah, right." Tyler stared across the square at Ellie's office, then turned to Roger and added, "Thanks for clarifying what went down last night."

"No problem. Thanks for not decking me." With a quick

wave, he walked away.

Tyler took out his phone and dialed Ellie's office. When Melody picked up, he asked, "What's the word on Frank?"

"Hey, Tyler. He's okay. Ellie's going to see him up this afternoon. I'm relieved you're in the loop. I wasn't sure she'd told anyone. You know how contained she can be."

"I do know," he said drily. "How's she doing?"

"Tired and stressed. I wish I could tell you more, but we've been dealing with patients since first thing this morning. We haven't had much chance to talk. I'd let you speak to her, but she's in with someone right now and if she doesn't finish soon she's not going to get ten lousy minutes to sit down and eat lunch. Want me to leave her a message you called?"

"No, that's okay." He didn't want to squeeze the things he had to say to her in between patients or a trip to Lexington to visit her father. "I'll catch up with her later."

"I think she'll be back from Lexington after six, if you want to try her then."

"Thanks, Mel." He glanced at his watch and did some quick figuring. He could do better than a phone call at six if he got his ass in gear.

· · ·

Ellie plopped into her chair and stifled a groan when she checked the patient schedule on her desk. Busy was good, she reminded herself, but a fifteen-minute lunch break she was five minutes late starting wouldn't do much for her headache and sagging energy. Or her hunger. She needed food and was contemplating her options—a candy bar or a bag of pretzels from the snack stash in her desk drawer—when Melody knocked on the open door and came in carrying a to-go bag from DeShay's.

She set the bag down front and center on Ellie's desk. "I

took the liberty of ordering you a turkey and Swiss on wheat."

Ellie's stomach growled its approval. "I'm giving you a raise," she said, digging into the bag. "A big one. Name your price."

The blonde laughed and perched on the corner of the desk. "Let's see how this month's receipts look and then we'll talk. Speaking of talking, I spoke to Roger last night."

Unsure what to say, Ellie concentrated on opening the sandwich wrapper and spreading it out into a makeshift place mat.

"He told me he came out to you, and you were incredibly understanding and supportive."

"That's sweet of him to say, but I reacted like any friend would."

"Not in his mind. He's got this deep-seated fear everybody will loathe him if they know the truth, so he hasn't opened up to many people. I've tried to convince him otherwise, but my assurances only go so far." She paused, and took a deep breath. "Can you forgive me for not telling you about Roger? I promised him I wouldn't tell a soul."

"There's nothing to forgive. It's not your fault I refused to see several huge signs that were staring me right in the face."

Melody brushed that aside with a wave of her hand. "Sometimes the journey to love involves some bumpy detours, as any girl with a gay ex-fiancé will tell you. But I've learned a smooth trip isn't particularly important. Getting there is what matters."

"Are you getting there?"

She smiled and nodded. "Yes, I believe I am, finally. Josh makes an excellent guide. He keeps me on the right path."

"I'm glad," Ellie said, meaning it. "Send me a postcard from happily ever after, because I don't think I'm making the trip anytime soon."

Melody stood and strolled to the door. At the threshold,

she turned and gave Ellie an odd look. "Something tells me you're not as far away as you think."

Before Ellie could reply, the bell dinged from the waiting room, signaling the arrival of the next patient. She started to get up, but Melody stopped her. "Eat. I've got to get new insurance information and take care of the co-pay. Don't worry, I'll get you out of here on time."

"Have I mentioned a raise lately?"

Melody laughed as she walked away. "Yeah, you have."

• • •

Ellie bounced like a pinball between exam rooms all afternoon, seeing patients, writing prescriptions, updating charts...and yet somehow still found time to obsess over Tyler. Should she call him and try to explain herself, or stop by his place so they could speak face-to-face? What, exactly, should she say to him? *When I asked you to teach me how to be wilder in bed, I wanted to turn myself into Roger's fantasy woman. I never dreamed I'd end up falling in love with you.* If the "I love you" part didn't send him running for the hills, the "turn myself into Roger's fantasy woman" would. *God, Ellie,* she scrubbed a hand over her tired eyes and stifled a noise somewhere between a whimper and a groan. *What the hell were you thinking?*

Certainly not that spending time with Tyler would be so easy, so effortless, and so addictive. She'd been physically attracted to him from the start, but his sexy smile and easy charm had distracted her from the strength of his character and the capacity of his heart. She hadn't expected to find a friend, a confidant, a soul mate. She hadn't expected to find love.

The half hour spent driving to Lexington to check on Frank brought her no closer to figuring out how to explain herself. Their visit offered no chance to sort through her muddled thoughts because Frank spent the entire time complaining about lousy hospital food and bloodsucking nurses. But hey, at least they were talking.

While she was there, Sharon stopped by with a get well soon gift—a diabetic cookbook. Sharon and Frank sat together on the bed, leafing through the book. Frank insisted every entrée looked "like crap," but Sharon kept at him, and before long, had him talked into trying one with her as soon as his hospital stay ended. Ellie said goodbye and headed out. Her dad was in good hands, and she had her own issues to tackle, starting with the screwed-up mess of her love life.

She rehearsed what to say to Tyler on the drive home. First off, she owed him an explanation as to why she'd been kissing Roger yesterday evening. That was a relatively easy conversation, compared to the thornier things she had to confess. Maybe Tyler didn't care—they never discussed exclusivity, after all—but it mattered to her. She wanted him to know the whole truth. He deserved to know the truth, including her real motive for seeking sexual experience, no matter how sadly misguided she'd been. Hand-in-hand with the explanation about Roger, she owed him an apology for manipulating him into helping her with such a crass, calculated pursuit. Once she got all that out on the table, the chance he'd believe she'd developed genuine feelings for him, or was even capable of genuine feelings, seemed remote. *Hi, I spent the last few weeks using you to help me win another man's heart, but now I realize I don't love him—I love you.* He'd probably crack a rib laughing at her.

She parked her car in the driveway and headed to her front door, still deep in thought, and drew up short when she saw Tyler sitting on her porch steps. For a second, she simply drank in the sight of him while her heart skipped around in her chest. Belatedly, she noticed his truck parked in her driveway, between the house and the garage.

"Tyler...what are you doing here?"

He slowly got to his feet, eyes never leaving her face. "How's your dad?"

"How did you know—?"

"It's a small town. Word travels."

Clearly, it did. Was that why he'd come? To ask about Frank? She approached the porch, trying without much success to get a read on his mood. As usual he exuded calm and his expression gave nothing away.

"Frank's okay. Mismanaging his diabetes landed him in the ER, but if there's a bright side to a night in the hospital, he seems to be taking his disease seriously. Also, he joined AA."

Her voice held steady, but her heartbeat refused to normalize. The weight of everything she wanted to say threatened to crush her.

"Good. I hope he follows through."

"Me, too." Holding his clear, steady gaze, she found herself diving clumsily into an unrehearsed topic. "He told me about the 'options' you gave him."

Those green eyes flashed. "I'm not going to apologize for stepping in."

"I'm not asking you to. I've been trying to convince him to stop drinking for years and never made any headway. You succeeded in getting him to meetings with a single conversation. Obviously—" She swallowed and concentrated on unlocking her door because tears stung her eyes. "Obviously, I should have asked for help a long time ago."

He placed a hand on her arm. "I had the right hammer at the right time, that's all, and I don't mean threatening to have him arrested. What really shook him was thinking I might actually convince you to cut him loose if he didn't get himself together. He wants you in his life, even if his pride won't allow him to say the words."

Twenty-four hours ago, she would have argued to the contrary, but after her father's apology last night, and his statements about making amends, she had to admit he seemed to be trying to repair their relationship. Not sure she could speak to say thank-you, she nodded and motioned for him to come inside. He picked up his computer bag from the porch step and followed her.

"Speaking of asking for help, you could have called me to drive to Lexington with you last night. I guess I haven't made this clear, but I'm here for you as more than just some sex tutor. You don't have to do everything by yourself."

She nodded and turned to face him. This side of him no longer surprised her. He stood up for people, supported his friends. "The call came so suddenly, I honestly didn't think about contacting anyone. Besides, you had the meeting with the bank to prepare for. I hope it went well."

"The meeting went fine. Junior dazzled them and we got the loan."

She grasped his hands before she could stop herself. "Congratulations. I know what this meant to you, and I'm glad they made the right decision." But now it occurred to her that he might be on her doorstep for reasons other than Frank, and she forced herself to loosen her grip on him. "I guess…I guess you're going to be pretty busy now, adding the Browning project to your slate."

"I am," he agreed. "Along with the Browning rehab, another priority arose—something I hadn't planned on and never saw coming. It requires I shift my focus immediately."

A lump wanted to form in her throat. She swallowed hard and nodded. She knew what was coming. Expected it. "I completely understand if you need to bow out of our last lesson."

Tyler gave her a small grin. "I was hoping you'd let the last one slide. There's nothing I can teach you anyway. You drive a man to his knees just fine as is. And, like I said, I've got this new priority."

His words pulled a strangled laugh from her. The only man she cared to drive to his knees stood before her, about to finalize his escape. "You went above and beyond the terms of our deal—one I never should have forced on you in the first place. I leveraged your loyalty to a friend for my own benefit, not to mention completely abused the doctor-patient relationship. I'm so sorry." On an uneven breath, she raised her eyes to his and added, "I hope one day you can forgive me."

"Shoot, Doc. You're making things awkward for me. I was kinda planning to turn the tables and ask for your help with something." His smile stayed in place, but his eyes went dark and serious.

She twisted her fingers together. "Anything, but what could I possibly help you with?"

"This new priority I mentioned involves my heart. I could really benefit from your expertise. I hoped to convince you to give me five lessons."

Air rushed from her lungs. Oh, God, a cardiac problem. Without conscious thought, she flattened her hand over his chest, her palm unerringly finding the steady, measured drum of his heart. He felt so strong, so vital. "What's the matter with your heart?" The question tumbled out in a harsh whisper.

"It's a little hard to explain, and I wasn't sure exactly what help I'd need, so I took a cue from someone I know who recently found herself in a similar situation. I consulted the experts." Before she could ask which specialists he'd seen, he reached into his computer bag and pulled out a book with five little green flags sticking neatly from the side, marking chapters. "Here," he handed the volume to her.

She turned the book over in her hand and glanced down at the cover, not really absorbing the words, then looked back at him. "Whatever diagnosis you've received, we can..." Wait, what was the book's title? She looked down again. *A Hundred and One Ways to Make Her Love You Forever.* "I don't understand."

"Simple, Doc. When you wanted to learn how to drive a man to his knees, you got yourself a book and a tutor. I need to figure out how to win a certain girl's heart and make her love me forever, and I want you to coach me. In fact, I consider your participation essential."

Her heart turned to lead and dropped straight into her stomach. She deserved this, undoubtedly, and silently congratulated fate or karma or whatever on the painfully ironic payback. So much for convincing Tyler she loved him. During the weeks she'd wasted ignoring and subjugating her feelings for him, he'd gone and fallen for someone else. Unfortunately, all the cosmic justice in the universe wouldn't help her pull off his request. No way.

Blindly, she thrust the book at him. "I can't. I'm sorry. Ask someone else. I know I said I'd do anything you needed, but when you said you had a problem with your heart, I thought you meant a health problem." She stared at the buttons on his white shirt and took a moment to get herself under control before adding, "Besides, you don't need any help winning hearts. Any girl would be lucky to have yours."

He tipped her chin until she met his gaze. The corner of his mouth crooked into a half-smile. "Apparently not. I've been trying to win yours for a while now and I don't seem to be getting the job done."

Her brain refused to cooperate with her vocal chords. He simply smiled down at her, patiently.

"Mine?" she finally whispered.

"Yeah, yours. So, you see..." He placed the book on her

entryway table and caught her wrists, pulling her in close. "It doesn't make much sense for me to practice with anyone else."

Joy surged through her and swept her anxiety and uncertainty away. She hugged him tight, reveling in the feel of his arms around her, the warmth of his chest under her cheek. When she pulled back, she looked him in the eye.

"You're right, it doesn't. Especially since you don't need any practice at all. You already have my heart—probably have since the first night you showed up here with lipstick on your shirt and a bullet in your butt. But I was too fixated on my stupid plan for happily ever after to see the truth right in front of me. You're the man I want. The man I love. You're my happily ever—"

He cut her off with a kiss that made chapter 2 of the *Wild Woman* guide seem as exciting as a handshake. When her vision went gray at the edges and her head spun—either from the effects of the kiss or the need for oxygen—he lifted his head.

"I love you, Ellie. I know I'm not the upstanding Prince Charming you always dreamed of—"

"The thing about Prince Charming is, he doesn't exist. He's a fantasy for little girls." Now she lost her battle with the tears. They welled and flowed, and probably tracked mascara down her face, but she really didn't care because what she wanted to say was way more important. "You're the real thing—a grown woman's fantasy—sexy, unpredictable, a little bit of a bad boy, but decent to the core. You're everything I want. You're everything I need. I've outgrown fairy tales."

Tyler hauled her up against him and cocked one dark eyebrow. "What about the *Wild Woman* guide? You outgrown that, too?"

"Um, I don't know. Why?" The question ended in a squeal when he swept her into his arms and strode down the hall toward her bedroom.

"We never knocked out chapter 9. I believe I mentioned it's one of my personal favorites."

She gave him her best seductive smolder, despite the fact that between the tears and the mascara she probably looked like a raccoon. "Does it drive you to your knees?"

"*You* drive me to my knees. Always will."

He dropped her on the bed and kissed her again. "I'm planning to spend the rest of my life proving it to you," he said against her lips.

She laughed and pulled him down to her. "Start now."

Acknowledgments

You only get to be a debut author once. It's kind of like losing your virginity, but with slightly less tequila, and *a lot* more people. Bear with me, because I want to thank everyone who made "my first time" such an amazing, thrilling experience (the book, I mean). Big, sloppy thank-you kisses to...

My husband for not calling a lawyer or a psychiatrist when I told him I wanted to quit my job and become a writer.

My little guy for introducing me to the joys of motherhood...and Lunchables.

Sheila Tenold for reading a scary-rough draft of this story and saying, "Go for it!"

The lovely Maggie Kelley for constant, genuine positivity I could only hope to emulate through the use of highly controlled substances.

To my writing mentor, Lynne Marshall, and my fellow Entangled authors Robin Bielman and Hayson Manning, for preparing me in ways I didn't even realize for the next part of the writing journey.

Cari Quinn, for 1) being Cari Quinn; and 2) the nice stuff

you said on the cover.

Indefatigable Sue Winegardner...all-night reader, speed-editor, logic-checker, REALITY checker.

Heather Howland, for saying "Yes!"; for telling me what questions to ask, and then answering them; and, oh yeah, for a cover straight out of my wildest dreams. It's like you're in my head—sorry about that.

And, last but never least, to Mom.

About the Author

USA TODAY bestselling author Samanthe Beck lives in Malibu, California, with her husband, their son, Kitty the furry Ninja, and Bebe the trash talkin' Chihuahua. When not writing fun and sexy contemporary romance, or napping on her beach towel with her face snuggled to her Kindle, she searches for the perfect ten dollar wine to pair with Lunchables.

Connect with Sam via Facebook, Twitter, or through her website at www.samanthebeck.com to check her progress on that never-ending quest, or to get the latest on her upcoming Brazens!

Made in the USA
Las Vegas, NV
06 December 2022